MRS. SPRING FRAGRANCE AND OTHER WRITINGS

MRS. SPRING FRAGRANCE

AND OTHER WRITINGS

SUI SIN FAR

Introduction by C Pam Zhang

MODERN LIBRARY

NEW YORK

2021 Modern Library Trade Paperback Edition
Introduction copyright © 2021 by C Pam Zhang

Published in the United States by Modern Library, an imprint
of Random House, a division of Penguin Random House LLC,
New York.

MODERN LIBRARY and the TORCHBEARER colophon are
registered trademarks of Penguin Random House LLC.

ISBN 978-0-593-24120-2
Ebook ISBN 978-0-593-24121-9

Printed in the United States of America on acid-free paper

modernlibrary.com

randomhousebooks.com

2 4 6 8 9 7 5 3 1

CONTENTS

Introduction by C Pam Zhang	vii
MRS. SPRING FRAGRANCE	3
THE INFERIOR WOMAN	16
THE WISDOM OF THE NEW	32
"ITS WAVERING IMAGE"	54
THE GIFT OF LITTLE ME	61
THE STORY OF ONE WHITE WOMAN WHO MARRIED A CHINESE	70
HER CHINESE HUSBAND	83
THE AMERICANIZING OF PAU TSU	90
IN THE LAND OF THE FREE	101
THE CHINESE LILY	112
THE SMUGGLING OF TIE CO	116
THE GOD OF RESTORATION	122
THE THREE SOULS OF AH SO NAN	128
THE PRIZE CHINA BABY	136
LIN JOHN	140
TIAN SHAN'S KINDRED SPIRIT	143
THE SING SONG WOMAN	150
Leaves from the Mental Portfolio of an Eurasian	155

INTRODUCTION

BY C PAM ZHANG

"I desire to write an immortal book," announces the character Mrs. Spring Fragrance, in one of the first stories of this collection. It stopped me cold, that beguiling phrase. What does it mean for a book to be immortal?

This question permeates the life and work of Mrs. Spring Fragrance's creator, Sui Sin Far, born Edith Maude Eaton, a woman acutely aware of her role as one of the first North American writers of Chinese heritage. One path to immortality is through myths and parables—the first stories, which Far loved. While this collection is set in San Francisco and Seattle at the turn of the twentieth century, I am not reminded of realist fiction so much as of Greek myths and Aesop's fables. Far's stories have that speed, that cadence, that resounding thud of a moral message hitting the floor. Characters are painted in broad, familiar brushstrokes: sweet young wives, rich men, poor strivers, precocious children, star-crossed lovers. Events unfold swiftly, in high color. Reading of the fiery death of a crippled girl, or of a mother who poisons her son in a tragic act of misunderstanding, I feel the thrill of encountering those quintessential Greek tragedies. Far's stories are meant for grand stages, the characters larger than life.

Myths and fables are created to instruct. Wise elders pass them to attention-deficient students, the shiny words enclosing basic lessons: this is how to behave in a society, this is what it looks like to be a person. And so when I read a sentence like "Now Tian Shan, being Chinese, had never saved money and, therefore, had no home," I am brought back to the simplicity of a fable that explains, just as deftly, that tortoises are slow and steady, or that Anansi the spider is clever.

Heavy-handed, yet effective. You can almost see the machinery turn as the story educates its reader. In this case the reader was the white American in 1912, and Far's moral was that the Chinese are human.

If this lesson seems obvious or cringey to a twenty-first century sensibility, then that is not a criticism of the writer so much as of the world she lived in. Sui Sin Far was a woman ahead of her time. Born in 1865 to a Chinese British mother and a white American father, she predated the term "biracial," which was coined in the 1890s, as well as the idea of the "white gaze," which was popularized in the late twentieth century. Far died in 1914. Imagine, if you can, what it was like to live as a half-Chinese girl in a time before a globalized view of identity, before Facebook and Meetup groups connected you to others like yourself, when rampant anti-Chinese sentiment in North America was codified in laws that restricted Chinese immigration, property ownership, paths to citizenship, and marriage. Thus isolated, Far worked within the inadequate constraints of existing language to define herself—which she did, admirably.

As a child, Far fantasized about dying a martyr so that, over her body, someone might trumpet, "Behold, how great and glorious and noble are the Chinese people!" The characters in *Mrs. Spring Fragrance and Other Stories* are so noble as to be godlike. A crippled girl sacrifices herself so that her brother can be with the woman he loves. Young parents suffer bravely and irreproachably through the lawful abduction of their newborn son by the United States government under the Chinese Exclusion Act of 1882, which was not repealed until either 1943 or much later, depending on how you see it.* There is hardly a speck of moral gray to be found in the Chinese

---

* The Magnuson Act of 1943, passed two years after China became an allied nation to the United States in World War II, allowed just 105 Chinese immigrants to enter each year. The Immigration and Nationality Act of 1952 abolished direct racial restrictions for immigration. However, a significant increase in Chinese immigration did not occur until after the passage of the Immigration and Nationality Act of 1965, which ended use of the National Origins formula that restricted immigration from what were considered less desirable parts of the world: Southern Europe, Eastern Europe, and Asia.

of Far's fictional world. They must be almost superhuman to counterbalance the racist stereotypes of the real world, in which the Chinese are casually derided as "subhuman" by a white acquaintance of Far's. "The Chinese in America owe an everlasting debt of gratitude to Sui Sin Far for the bold stance she has taken in their defense," a Chinese businessman wrote.

And so Far's Chinese characters often feel trapped in a mold: forcedly good, as well as forcedly Chinese. Over and over we are hit with this binary. "Don't you see that you have got to decide what you will be—Chinese or white?" "Chinese character is wonderful." "The poor little thing became more of an American" is said of a young Chinese bride in *The Wisdom of the New,* where Americanness refers to the knotty emotion of jealousy—Chineseness, we are made to understand, is pure and unconflicted. Yet the Chinese bride is not allowed to fully inhabit that jealousy; we are soon made to understand that she is an innocent victim of circumstance.

Perhaps the most satisfyingly nuanced character, then, is the white woman who narrates *Her Chinese Husband.* Here is that juicy ambiguity I crave. Though she loves her husband, the unnamed narrator wrestles with ingrained stereotypes about dominant races and second wives, and wonders, "between us—that strange, invisible— what? Was it the barrier of race—that consciousness?" The white woman's unredacted thoughts are a welcome blast of cold air when all that nobility gets a little stifling. By contrast, when we tunnel inside the head of a Chinese husband in *The Wisdom of the New,* we hit again the smooth, impenetrable wall of superhuman goodness: "He felt himself exiled from Paradise, yet it did not occur to him to question, as a white man would have done, whether the angel with the flaming sword had authority . . . He simply made up his mind to make the best of what was."

My god, do I want him to snatch that sword. I want to see the Chinese husband liberated from the straightjacket of nobility; I want him to question authority, to rise up as messy, violent, injured, petty, *real.* The moral cleanliness of Far's characters can hurt in the way that it hurts to stare too long at a field of pure, white snow. But if I sting, then only imagine the agony Far suffered.

She was a woman, as I've said, ahead of her time. Rather than race forward alone, she chose to slow down and extend her hand to white Americans—so uneducated about the Chinese, so facile and childish in their bigotry—and write, for them, stories that would amuse even as they instructed. But if Far's fiction is pinned to the white American imagination of 1912, the essay that closes out this collection is a leap forward into time, into possibility. The high style of Far's fiction—flowery, dramatic, often purpled with Orientalist tropes of peaches and jade—loses its ornaments as the writer recounts her lifelong experiences of racism and alienation. She does not sugarcoat her personal story of hearing Chinese people compared to pigs; she does not provide a neat moral lesson in her account of being sexually solicited due to her race. In the relaxing of Far's prose I sense the relief of a writer setting down a burden, as if she is saying, here are the facts, it is not my job to beautify them for you. It is a steelier and more acerbic writer who declares, "I cheer myself with the fact that I am but a pioneer. A pioneer should glory in suffering."

I want to return to the *immortal book* that Mrs. Spring Fragrance mentions. This is, in many ways, the opposite of the book Sui Sin Far wrote. The fictional Mrs. Spring Fragrance—a Chinese woman thriving in San Francisco—intends to write about the foibles of her white American friends; she is laughing, lovingly, at them. There are wonderful moments in which you can hear Far laughing, too. I cackled at a passage in which Mrs. Spring Fragrance slyly dismantles a pretentious lecture on "America, the Protector of China!" How many white Americans in 1912, I wonder, picked up on the irony? How many white Americans were meant to? It wasn't written for them. It is a joke lobbed through the decades at me, a Chinese American woman in 2021, sick of reading tropes of delicate flowers and jade pendants. It is utterly electrifying. Far was ahead of her time; she was a time traveler.

I offer one final Greek myth: Prometheus, who gave fire to humanity and paid in his own flesh. Sui Sin Far gave us the first book on the Chinese in America—the immortal book, instructive as fables should be. In doing so she helped pave the way for writers like myself to smash stereotypes, push past white audiences, laugh at our own jokes, and write books for other Chinese Americans first. I don't mean to deride noble acts, which certainly exist. Far was noble when she took it upon herself to affirm the humanity of an entire race. Yet I can't help but wonder—what would Far have written if she did not have to be noble, if she did not live her life thinking that martyrdom was necessary to make white people listen? "I fail to make myself intelligible," she writes of her attempt, as a four-year-old, to describe her first brush with racism. But it is always a question of intelligible to whom. I can't help but fantasize about transporting a writer like Sui Sin Far, ahead of her time, into the modern day, and saying to her: Forget those people, talk to me. I'm listening. I understand.

Here is how we listen. We read her.

———

Born in Beijing, C PAM ZHANG is mostly an artifact of the United States. She is the author of *How Much of These Hills Is Gold,* winner of the Asian/Pacific American Award for Literature, a finalist for the PEN/Hemingway Award, and longlisted for the Booker Prize. Zhang is a National Book Foundation 5 Under 35 Honoree.

MRS. SPRING FRAGRANCE AND OTHER WRITINGS

MRS. SPRING FRAGRANCE

I

When Mrs. Spring Fragrance first arrived in Seattle, she was unacquainted with even one word of the American language. Five years later her husband, speaking of her, said: "There are no more American words for her learning." And everyone who knew Mrs. Spring Fragrance agreed with Mr. Spring Fragrance.

Mr. Spring Fragrance, whose business name was Sing Yook, was a young curio merchant. Though conservatively Chinese in many respects, he was at the same time what is called by the Westerners, "Americanized." Mrs. Spring Fragrance was even more "Americanized."

Next door to the Spring Fragrances lived the Chin Yuens. Mrs. Chin Yuen was much older than Mrs. Spring Fragrance; but she had a daughter of eighteen with whom Mrs. Spring Fragrance was on terms of great friendship. The daughter was a pretty girl whose Chinese name was Mai Gwi Far (a rose) and whose American name was Laura. Nearly everybody called her Laura, even her parents and Chinese friends. Laura had a sweetheart, a youth named Kai Tzu. Kai Tzu, who was American-born, and as ruddy and stalwart as any young Westerner, was noted, amongst baseball players, as one of the finest pitchers on the Coast. He could also sing, "Drink to me only with thine eyes," to Laura's piano accompaniment.

Now the only person who knew that Kai Tzu loved Laura and that Laura loved Kai Tzu, was Mrs. Spring Fragrance. The reason for this was that, although the Chin Yuen parents lived in a house furnished in American style, and wore American clothes, yet they religiously observed many Chinese customs, and their ideals of life were the ideals of their Chinese forefathers. Therefore, they had betrothed their daughter, Laura, at the age of fifteen, to the eldest son of the Chinese Government schoolteacher in San Francisco. The time for the consummation of the betrothal was approaching.

Laura was with Mrs. Spring Fragrance and Mrs. Spring Fragrance was trying to cheer her.

"I had such a pretty walk today," said she. "I crossed the banks above the beach and came back by the long road. In the green grass the daffodils were blowing, in the cottage gardens the currant bushes were flowering, and in the air was the perfume of the wallflower. I wished, Laura, that you were with me."

Laura burst into tears. "That is the walk," she sobbed, "Kai Tzu and I so love; but never, ah, never, can we take it together again."

"Now, Little Sister," comforted Mrs. Spring Fragrance, "you really must not grieve like that. Is there not a beautiful American poem written by a noble American named Tennyson, which says:

"*'Tis better to have loved and lost,*
Than never to have loved at all?"

Mrs. Spring Fragrance was unaware that Mr. Spring Fragrance, having returned from the city, tired with the day's business, had thrown himself down on the bamboo settee on the veranda, and that although his eyes were engaged in scanning the pages of the *Chinese World*, his ears could not help receiving the words which were borne to him through the open window.

"*'Tis better to have loved and lost,*
Than never to have loved at all,"

repeated Mr. Spring Fragrance. Not wishing to hear more of the secret talk of women, he arose and sauntered around the veranda to the other side of the house. Two pigeons circled around his head. He felt in his pocket for a lychee which he usually carried for their pecking. His fingers touched a little box. It contained a jadestone pendant, which Mrs. Spring Fragrance had particularly admired the last time she was downtown. It was the fifth anniversary of Mr. and Mrs. Spring Fragrance's wedding day.

Mr. Spring Fragrance pressed the little box down into the depths of his pocket.

A young man came out of the back door of the house at Mr. Spring Fragrance's left. The Chin Yuen house was at his right.

"Good evening," said the young man. "Good evening," returned Mr. Spring Fragrance. He stepped down from his porch and went and leaned over the railing which separated this yard from the yard in which stood the young man.

"Will you please tell me," said Mr. Spring Fragrance, "the meaning of two lines of an American verse which I have heard?"

"Certainly," returned the young man with a genial smile. He was a star student at the University of Washington, and had not the slightest doubt that he could explain the meaning of all things in the universe.

"Well," said Mr. Spring Fragrance, "it is this:

"'Tis better to have loved and lost,
Than never to have loved at all."

"Ah!" responded the young man with an air of profound wisdom. "That, Mr. Spring Fragrance, means that it is a good thing to love anyway—even if we can't get what we love, or, as the poet tells us, lose what we love. Of course, one needs experience to feel the truth of this teaching."

The young man smiled pensively and reminiscently. More than a dozen young maidens "loved and lost" were passing before his mind's eye.

"The truth of the teaching!" echoed Mr. Spring Fragrance, a little testily. "There is no truth in it whatever. It is disobedient to reason. Is it not better to have what you do not love than to love what you do not have?"

"That depends," answered the young man, "upon temperament."

"I thank you. Good evening," said Mr. Spring Fragrance. He turned away to muse upon the unwisdom of the American way of looking at things.

Meanwhile, inside the house, Laura was refusing to be comforted.

"Ah, no! no!" cried she. "If I had not gone to school with Kai Tzu, nor talked nor walked with him, nor played the accompaniments to his songs, then I might consider with complacency, or at least without horror, my approaching marriage with the son of Man You. But as it is—oh, as it is—!"

The girl rocked herself to and fro in heartfelt grief.

Mrs. Spring Fragrance knelt down beside her, and clasping her arms around her neck, cried in sympathy:

"Little Sister, oh, Little Sister! Dry your tears—do not despair. A moon has yet to pass before the marriage can take place. Who knows what the stars may have to say to one another during its passing? A little bird has whispered to me—"

For a long time Mrs. Spring Fragrance talked. For a long time Laura listened. When the girl arose to go, there was a bright light in her eyes.

II

Mrs. Spring Fragrance, in San Francisco on a visit to her cousin, the wife of the herb doctor of Clay Street, was having a good time. She was invited everywhere that the wife of an honorable Chinese merchant could go. There was much to see and hear, including more than a dozen babies who had been born in the families of her friends since she last visited the city of the Golden Gate. Mrs. Spring Fragrance loved babies. She had had two herself, but both had been transplanted into the spirit land before the completion of even one moon. There were also many dinners and theater parties given in her honor. It was at one of the theater parties that Mrs. Spring Fragrance met Ah Oi, a young girl who had the reputation of being the prettiest Chinese girl in San Francisco, and the naughtiest. In spite of gossip, however, Mrs. Spring Fragrance took a great fancy to Ah Oi and invited her to a tête-à-tête picnic on the following day. This invitation Ah Oi joyfully accepted. She was a sort of bird girl and never felt so happy as when out in the park or woods.

On the day after the picnic Mrs. Spring Fragrance wrote to Laura Chin Yuen thus:

My Precious Laura,—*May the bamboo ever wave. Next week I accompany Ah Oi to the beauteous town of San Jose. There will we be met by the son of the Illustrious Teacher, and in a little Mission, presided over by a benevolent American priest, the little Ah Oi and the son of the Illustrious Teacher will be joined together in love and harmony—two pieces of music made to complete one another.*

The Son of the Illustrious Teacher, having been through an American Hall of Learning, is well able to provide for his orphan bride and fears not the displeasure of his parents, now that he is assured that your grief at his loss will not be inconsolable. He wishes me to waft to you and to Kai Tzu—and the little Ah Oi joins with him—ten thousand rainbow wishes for your happiness.

My respects to your honorable parents, and to yourself, the heart of your loving friend,

Jade Spring Fragrance

To Mr. Spring Fragrance, Mrs. Spring Fragrance also indited a letter:

Great and Honored Man,—*Greeting from your plum blossom,* who is desirous of hiding herself from the sun of your presence for a week of seven days more. My honorable cousin is preparing for the Fifth Moon Festival, and wishes me to compound for the occasion some American "fudge," for which delectable sweet, made by my clumsy hands, you have sometimes shown a slight prejudice. I am enjoying a most agreeable*

---

* The plum blossom is the Chinese flower of virtue. It has been adopted by the Japanese, just in the same way as they have adopted the Chinese national flower, the chrysanthemum.

visit, and American friends, as also our own, strive benevolently for the accomplishment of my pleasure. Mrs. Samuel Smith, an American lady, known to my cousin, asked for my accompaniment to a magniloquent lecture the other evening. The subject was "America, the Protector of China!" It was most exhilarating, and the effect of so much expression of benevolence leads me to beg of you to forget to remember that the barber charges you one dollar for a shave while he humbly submits to the American man a bill of fifteen cents. And murmur no more because your honored elder brother, on a visit to this country, is detained under the roof-tree of this great Government instead of under your own humble roof. Console him with the reflection that he is protected under the wing of the Eagle, the Emblem of Liberty. What is the loss of ten hundred years or ten thousand times ten dollars compared with the happiness of knowing oneself so securely sheltered? All of this I have learned from Mrs. Samuel Smith, who is as brilliant and great of mind as one of your own superior sex.

For me it is sufficient to know that the Golden Gate Park is most enchanting, and the seals on the rock at the Cliff House extremely entertaining and amiable. There is much feasting and merry-making under the lanterns in honor of your Stupid Thorn.

I have purchased for your smoking a pipe with an amber mouth. It is said to be very sweet to the lips and to emit a cloud of smoke fit for the gods to inhale.

Awaiting, by the wonderful wire of the telegram message, your gracious permission to remain for the celebration of the Fifth Moon Festival and the making of American "fudge," I continue for ten thousand times ten thousand years,

Your ever loving and obedient woman,
Jade

P.S. Forget not to care for the cat, the birds, and the flowers. Do not eat too quickly nor fan too vigorously now that the weather is warming.

Mrs. Spring Fragrance smiled as she folded this last epistle. Even if he were old-fashioned, there was never a husband so good and kind as hers. Only on one occasion since their marriage had he slighted her wishes. That was when, on the last anniversary of their wedding, she had signified a desire for a certain jadestone pendant, and he had failed to satisfy that desire.

But Mrs. Spring Fragrance, being of a happy nature, and disposed to look upon the bright side of things, did not allow her mind to dwell upon the jadestone pendant. Instead, she gazed complacently down upon her bejeweled fingers and folded in with her letter to Mr. Spring Fragrance a bright little sheaf of condensed love.

III

Mr. Spring Fragrance sat on his doorstep. He had been reading two letters, one from Mrs. Spring Fragrance, and the other from an elderly bachelor cousin in San Francisco. The one from the elderly bachelor cousin was a business letter, but contained the following postscript:

> *Tsen Hing, the son of the Government schoolmaster, seems to be much in the company of your young wife. He is a good-looking youth, and pardon me, my dear cousin; but if women are allowed to stray at will from under their husbands' mulberry roofs, what is to prevent them from becoming butterflies?*

"Sing Foon is old and cynical," said Mr. Spring Fragrance to himself. "Why should I pay any attention to him? This is America, where a man may speak to a woman, and a woman listen, without any thought of evil."

He destroyed his cousin's letter and reread his wife's. Then he became very thoughtful. Was the making of American fudge sufficient reason for a wife to wish to remain a week longer in a city where her husband was not?

The young man who lived in the next house came out to water the lawn.

"Good evening," said he. "Any news from Mrs. Spring Fragrance?"

"She is having a very good time," returned Mr. Spring Fragrance.

"Glad to hear it. I think you told me she was to return the end of this week."

"I have changed my mind about her," said Mr. Spring Fragrance. "I am bidding her remain a week longer, as I wish to give a smoking party during her absence. I hope I may have the pleasure of your company."

"I shall be delighted," returned the young fellow. "But, Mr. Spring Fragrance, don't invite any other white fellows. If you do not I shall be able to get in a scoop. You know, I'm a sort of honorary reporter for the *Gleaner*."

"Very well," absently answered Mr. Spring Fragrance.

"Of course, your friend the Consul will be present. I shall call it 'A high-class Chinese stag party!'"

In spite of his melancholy mood, Mr. Spring Fragrance smiled.

"Everything is 'high-class' in America," he observed.

"Sure!" cheerfully assented the young man. "Haven't you ever heard that all Americans are princes and princesses, and just as soon as a foreigner puts his foot upon our shores, he also becomes of the nobility—I mean, the royal family."

"What about my brother in the Detention Pen?" dryly inquired Mr. Spring Fragrance.

"Now you've got me," said the young man, rubbing his head. "Well, that is a shame—'a beastly shame,' as the Englishman says. But understand, old fellow, we that are real Americans are up against that—even more than you. It is against our principles."

"I offer the real Americans my consolations that they should be compelled to do that which is against their principles."

"Oh, well, it will all come right someday. We're not a bad sort, you know. Think of the indemnity money returned to the Dragon by Uncle Sam."

Mr. Spring Fragrance puffed his pipe in silence for some moments. More than politics was troubling his mind.

At last he spoke. "Love," said he, slowly and distinctly, "comes before the wedding in this country, does it not?"

"Yes, certainly."

Young Carman knew Mr. Spring Fragrance well enough to receive with calmness his most astounding queries.

"Presuming," continued Mr. Spring Fragrance—"presuming that some friend of your father's, living—presuming—in England—has a daughter that he arranges with your father to be your wife. Presuming that you have never seen that daughter, but that you marry her, knowing her not. Presuming that she marries you, knowing you not.—After she marries you and knows you, will that woman love you?"

"Emphatically, no," answered the young man.

"That is the way it would be in America—that the woman who marries the man like that—would not love him?"

"Yes, that is the way it would be in America. Love, in this country, must be free, or it is not love at all."

"In China, it is different!" mused Mr. Spring Fragrance.

"Oh, yes, I have no doubt that in China it is different."

"But the love is in the heart all the same," went on Mr. Spring Fragrance.

"Yes, all the same. Everybody falls in love sometime or another. Some"—pensively—"many times."

Mr. Spring Fragrance arose.

"I must go downtown," said he.

As he walked down the street he recalled the remark of a business acquaintance who had met his wife and had had some conversation with her: "She is just like an American woman."

He had felt somewhat flattered when this remark had been made. He looked upon it as a compliment to his wife's cleverness; but it rankled in his mind as he entered the telegraph office. If his wife was becoming as an American woman, would it not be possible for her to love as an American woman—a man to whom she was not married? There also floated in his memory the verse which his wife had quoted to the daughter of Chin Yuen. When the telegraph clerk handed him a blank, he wrote this message:

"Remain as you wish, but remember that ''Tis better to have loved and lost, than never to have loved at all.'"

—

When Mrs. Spring Fragrance received this message, her laughter tinkled like falling water. How droll! How delightful! Here was her husband quoting American poetry in a telegram. Perhaps he had been reading her American poetry books since she had left him! She hoped so. They would lead him to understand her sympathy for her dear Laura and Kai Tzu. She need no longer keep from him their secret. How joyful! It had been such a hardship to refrain from confiding in him before. But discreetness had been most necessary, seeing that Mr. Spring Fragrance entertained as old-fashioned, notions concerning marriage, as did the Chin Yuen parents. Strange that that should be so, since he had fallen in love with her picture before *ever* he had seen her, just as she had fallen in love with his! And when the marriage veil was lifted and each beheld the other for the first time in the flesh, there had been no disillusion—no lessening of the respect and affection, which those who had brought about the marriage had inspired in each young heart.

Mrs. Spring Fragrance began to wish she could fall asleep and wake to find the week flown, and she in her own little home pouring tea for Mr. Spring Fragrance.

IV

Mr. Spring Fragrance was walking to business with Mr. Chin Yuen. As they walked they talked. "Yes," said Mr. Chin Yuen, "the old order is passing away, and the new order is taking its place, even with us who are Chinese. I have finally consented to give my daughter in marriage to young Kai Tzu."

Mr. Spring Fragrance expressed surprise. He had understood that the marriage between his neighbor's daughter and the San Francisco schoolteacher's son was all arranged.

"So 'twas," answered Mr. Chin Yuen; "but it seems the young renegade, without consultation or advice, has placed his affections upon some untrustworthy female, and is so under her influence that he refuses to fulfil his parents' promise to me for him."

"So!" said Mr. Spring Fragrance. The shadow on his brow deepened.

"But," said Mr. Chin Yuen, with affable resignation, "it is all ordained by Heaven. Our daughter, as the wife of Kai Tzu, for whom she has long had a loving feeling, will not now be compelled to dwell with a mother-in-law and where her own mother is not. For that, we are thankful, as she is our only one and the conditions of life in this Western country are not as in China. Moreover, Kai Tzu, though not so much of a scholar as the teacher's son, has a keen eye for business and that, in America, is certainly much more desirable than scholarship. What do you think?"

"Eh! What!" exclaimed Mr. Spring Fragrance. The latter part of his companion's remarks had been lost upon him.

That day the shadow which had been following Mr. Spring Fragrance ever since he had heard his wife quote, "'Tis better to have loved," etc., became so heavy and deep that he quite lost himself within it.

At home in the evening he fed the cat, the bird, and the flowers. Then, seating himself in a carved black chair—a present from his wife on his last birthday—he took out his pipe and smoked. The cat jumped into his lap. He stroked it softly and tenderly. It had been much fondled by Mrs. Spring Fragrance, and Mr. Spring Fragrance was under the impression that it missed her. "Poor thing!" said he. "I suppose you want her back!" When he arose to go to bed he placed the animal carefully on the floor, and thus apostrophized it:

"O Wise and Silent One, your mistress returns to you, but her heart she leaves behind her, with the Tommies in San Francisco."

The Wise and Silent One made no reply. He was not a jealous cat.

Mr. Spring Fragrance slept not that night; the next morning he ate not. Three days and three nights without sleep and food went by.

There was a springlike freshness in the air on the day that Mrs. Spring Fragrance came home. The skies overhead were as blue as Puget Sound stretching its gleaming length toward the mighty Pacific, and all the beautiful green world seemed to be throbbing with Springing life.

Mrs. Spring Fragrance was never so radiant.

"Oh," she cried lightheartedly, "is it not lovely to see the sun shining so clear, and everything so bright to welcome me?"

Mr. Spring Fragrance made no response. It was the morning after the fourth sleepless night.

Mrs. Spring Fragrance noticed his silence, also his grave face.

"Everything—everyone is glad to see me but you," she declared, half seriously, half jestingly.

Mr. Spring Fragrance set down her valise. They had just entered the house.

"If my wife is glad to see me," he quietly replied, "I also am glad to see her!"

Summoning their servant boy, he bade him look after Mrs. Spring Fragrance's comfort.

"I must be at the store in half an hour," said he, looking at his watch. "There is some very important business requiring attention."

"What is the business?" inquired Mrs. Spring Fragrance, her lip quivering with disappointment.

"I cannot just explain to you," answered her husband.

Mrs. Spring Fragrance looked up into his face with honest and earnest eyes. There was something in his manner, in the tone of her husband's voice, which touched her.

"Yen," said she, "you do not look well. You are not well. What is it?"

Something arose in Mr. Spring Fragrance's throat which prevented him from replying.

"O darling one! O sweetest one!" cried a girl's joyous voice. Laura Chin Yuen ran into the room and threw her arms around Mrs. Spring Fragrance's neck.

"I spied you from the window," said Laura, "and I couldn't rest until I told you. We are to be married next week, Kai Tzu and I. And all through you, all through you—the sweetest jade jewel in the world!"

Mr. Spring Fragrance passed out of the room.

"So the son of the Government teacher and little Happy Love

are already married," Laura went on, relieving Mrs. Spring Fragrance of her cloak, her hat, and her folding fan.

Mr. Spring Fragrance paused upon the doorstep.

"Sit down, Little Sister, and I will tell you all about it," said Mrs. Spring Fragrance, forgetting her husband for a moment.

When Laura Chin Yuen had danced away, Mr. Spring Fragrance came in and hung up his hat.

"You got back very soon," said Mrs. Spring Fragrance, covertly wiping away the tears which had begun to fall as soon as she thought herself alone.

"I did not go," answered Mr. Spring Fragrance. "I have been listening to you and Laura."

"But if the business is very important, do not you think you should attend to it?" anxiously queried Mrs. Spring Fragrance.

"It is not important to me now," returned Mr. Spring Fragrance. "I would prefer to hear again about Ah Oi and Man You and Laura and Kai Tzu."

"How lovely of you to say that!" exclaimed Mrs. Spring Fragrance, who was easily made happy. And she began to chat away to her husband in the friendliest and wifeliest fashion possible. When she had finished she asked him if he were not glad to hear that those who loved as did the young lovers whose secrets she had been keeping, were to be united; and he replied that indeed he was; that he would like every man to be as happy with a wife as he himself had ever been and ever would be.

"You did not always talk like that," said Mrs. Spring Fragrance slyly. "You must have been reading my American poetry books!"

"American poetry!" ejaculated Mr. Spring Fragrance almost fiercely. "American poetry is detestable, *abhorrable!*"

"Why! why!" exclaimed Mrs. Spring Fragrance, more and more surprised.

But the only explanation which Mr. Spring Fragrance vouchsafed was a jadestone pendant.

THE INFERIOR WOMAN

I

Mrs. Spring Fragrance walked through the leafy alleys of the park, admiring the flowers and listening to the birds singing. It was a beautiful afternoon with the warmth from the sun cooled by a refreshing breeze. As she walked along she meditated upon a book which she had some notion of writing. Many American women wrote books. Why should not a Chinese? She would write a book about Americans for her Chinese women friends. The American people were so interesting and mysterious. Something of pride and pleasure crept into Mrs. Spring Fragrance's heart as she pictured Fei and Sie and Mai Gwi Far listening to Lae-Choo reading her illuminating paragraphs.

As she turned down a bypath she saw Will Carman, her American neighbor's son, coming toward her, and by his side a young girl who seemed to belong to the sweet air and brightness of all the things around her. They were talking very earnestly and the eyes of the young man were on the girl's face.

"Ah!" murmured Mrs. Spring Fragrance, after one swift glance. "It is love."

She retreated behind a syringa bush, which completely screened her from view.

Up the winding path went the young couple.

"It is love," repeated Mrs. Spring Fragrance, "and it is the 'Inferior Woman.'"

She had heard about the Inferior Woman from the mother of Will Carman.

After tea that evening Mrs. Spring Fragrance stood musing at her front window. The sun hovered over the Olympic mountains like a great, golden red-bird with dark purple wings, its long tail of light trailing underneath in the waters of Puget Sound.

"How very beautiful!" exclaimed Mrs. Spring Fragrance; then she sighed.

"Why do you sigh?" asked Mr. Spring Fragrance.

"My heart is sad," answered his wife.

"Is the cat sick?" inquired Mr. Spring Fragrance.

Mrs. Spring Fragrance shook her head. "It is not our Wise One who troubles me today," she replied. "It is our neighbors. The sorrow of the Carman household is that the mother desires for her son the Superior Woman, and his heart enshrines but the Inferior. I have seen them together today, and I know."

"What do you know?"

"That the Inferior Woman is the mate for young Carman."

Mr. Spring Fragrance elevated his brows. Only the day before, his wife's arguments had all been in favor of the Superior Woman. He uttered some words expressive of surprise, to which Mrs. Spring Fragrance retorted:

"Yesterday, O Great Man, I was a caterpillar!"

Just then young Carman came strolling up the path. Mr. Spring Fragrance opened the door to him. "Come in, neighbor," said he. "I have received some new books from Shanghai."

"Good," replied young Carman, who was interested in Chinese literature. While he and Mr. Spring Fragrance discussed *The Odes of Chow* and *The Sorrows of Han,* Mrs. Spring Fragrance, sitting in a low easy-chair of rose-colored silk, covertly studied her visitor's countenance. Why was his expression so much more grave than gay? It had not been so a year ago—before he had known the Inferior Woman. Mrs. Spring Fragrance noted other changes also, both in speech and manner. "He is no longer a boy," mused she. "He is a man, and it is the work of the Inferior Woman."

"And when, Mr. Carman," she inquired, "will you bring home a daughter to your mother?"

"And when, Mrs. Spring Fragrance, do you think I should?" returned the young man.

Mrs. Spring Fragrance spread wide her fan and gazed thoughtfully over its silver edge.

"The summer moons will soon be over," said she. "You should not wait until the grass is yellow."

> *"The woodmen's blows responsive ring,*
> *   As on the trees they fall,*
> *And when the birds their sweet notes sing,*
> *   They to each other call.*
> *From the dark valley comes a bird,*
> *   And seeks the lofty tree,*
> *Ying goes its voice, and thus it cries:*
> *   'Companion, come to me.'*
> *The bird, although a creature small*
> *   Upon its mate depends,*
> *And shall we men, who rank o'er all,*
> *   Not seek to have our friends?"*

quoted Mr. Spring Fragrance.

Mrs. Spring Fragrance tapped his shoulder approvingly with her fan.

"I perceive," said young Carman, "that you are both allied against my peace."

"It is for your mother," replied Mrs. Spring Fragrance soothingly. "She will be happy when she knows that your affections are fixed by marriage."

There was a slight gleam of amusement in the young man's eyes as he answered: "But if my mother has no wish for a daughter—at least, no wish for the daughter I would want to give her?"

"When I first came to America," returned Mrs. Spring Fragrance, "my husband desired me to wear the American dress. I protested and declared that never would I so appear. But one day he brought home a gown fit for a fairy, and ever since then I have worn and adored the American dress."

"Mrs. Spring Fragrance," declared young Carman, "your argument is incontrovertible."

II

A young man with a determined set to his shoulders stood outside the door of a little cottage perched upon a bluff overlooking the sound. The chill sea air was sweet with the scent of roses, and he drew in a deep breath of inspiration before he knocked.

"Are you not surprised to see me?" he inquired of the young person who opened the door.

"Not at all," replied the young person demurely.

He gave her a quick almost fierce look. At their last parting he had declared that he would not come again unless she requested him, and that she assuredly had not done.

"I wish I could make you feel," said he.

She laughed—a pretty infectious laugh which exorcised all his gloom. He looked down upon her as they stood together under the cluster of electric lights in her cozy little sitting-room. Such a slender, girlish figure! Such a soft cheek, red mouth, and firm little chin! Often in his dreams of her he had taken her into his arms and coaxed her into a good humor. But, alas! dreams are not realities, and the calm friendliness of this young person made any demonstration of tenderness well-nigh impossible. But for the shy regard of her eyes, you might have thought that he was no more to her than a friendly acquaintance.

"I hear," said she, taking up some needlework, "that your Welland case comes on tomorrow."

"Yes," answered the young lawyer, "and I have all my witnesses ready."

"So, I hear, has Mr. Greaves," she retorted. "You are going to have a hard fight."

"What of that, when in the end I'll win."

He looked over at her with a bright gleam in his eyes.

"I wouldn't be too sure," she warned demurely. "You may lose on a technicality."

He drew his chair a little nearer to her side and turned over the pages of a book lying on her worktable. On the flyleaf was inscribed in a man's writing: "To the dear little woman whose friendship is worth a fortune."

Another book beside it bore the inscription: "With the love of all the firm, including the boys," and a volume of poems above it was dedicated to the young person "with the high regards and stanch affection" of some other masculine person.

Will Carman pushed aside these evidences of his sweetheart's popularity with his own kind and leaned across the table.

"Alice," said he, "once upon a time you admitted that you loved me."

A blush suffused the young person's countenance.

"Did I?" she queried.

"You did, indeed."

"Well?"

"Well! If you love me and I love you—"

"Oh, please!" protested the girl, covering her ears with her hands.

"I *will* please," asserted the young man.

"I have come here tonight, Alice, to ask you to marry me—and at once."

"Deary me!" exclaimed the young person; but she let her needlework fall into her lap as her lover, approaching nearer, laid his arm around her shoulders and, bending his face close to hers, pleaded his most important case.

If for a moment the small mouth quivered, the firm little chin lost its firmness, and the proud little head yielded to the pressure of a lover's arm, it was only for a moment so brief and fleeting that Will Carman had hardly become aware of it before it had passed.

"No," said the young person sorrowfully but decidedly. She had arisen and was standing on the other side of the table facing him. "I cannot marry you while your mother regards me as beneath you."

"When she knows you she will acknowledge you are above me. But I am not asking you to come to my mother, I am asking you to come to me, dear. If you will put your hand in mine and trust to me through all the coming years, no man or woman born can come between us."

But the young person shook her head.

"No," she repeated. "I will not be your wife unless your mother welcomes me with pride and with pleasure."

The night air was still sweet with the perfume of roses as Will Carman passed out of the little cottage door; but he drew in no deep breath of inspiration. His impetuous Irish heart was too heavy with disappointment. It might have been a little lighter, however, had he known that the eyes of the young person who gazed after him were misty with a love and yearning beyond expression.

III

"Will Carman has failed to snare his bird," said Mr. Spring Fragrance to Mrs. Spring Fragrance.

Their neighbor's son had just passed their veranda without turning to bestow upon them his usual cheerful greeting.

"It is too bad," sighed Mrs. Spring Fragrance sympathetically. She clasped her hands together and exclaimed:

"Ah, these Americans! These mysterious, inscrutable, incomprehensible Americans! Had I the divine right of learning I would put them into an immortal book!"

"The divine right of learning," echoed Mr. Spring Fragrance. "Humph!"

Mrs. Spring Fragrance looked up into her husband's face in wonderment.

"Is not the authority of the scholar, the student, almost divine?" she queried.

"So 'tis said," responded he. "So it seems."

The evening before, Mr. Spring Fragrance, together with several

Seattle and San Francisco merchants, had given a dinner to a number of young students who had just arrived from China. The morning papers had devoted several columns to laudation of the students, prophecies as to their future, and the great influence which they would exercise over the destiny of their nation; but no comment whatever was made on the givers of the feast, and Mr. Spring Fragrance was therefore feeling somewhat unappreciated. Were not he and his brother merchants worthy of a little attention? If the students had come to learn things in America, they, the merchants, had accomplished things. There were those amongst them who had been instrumental in bringing several of the students to America. One of the boys was Mr. Spring Fragrance's own young brother, for whose maintenance and education he had himself sent the wherewithal every year for many years. Mr. Spring Fragrance, though well read in the Chinese classics, was not himself a scholar. As a boy he had come to the shores of America, worked his way up, and by dint of painstaking study after working hours acquired the Western language and Western business ideas. He had made money, saved money, and sent money home. The years had flown, his business had grown. Through his efforts, trade between his native town and the port city in which he lived had greatly increased. A school in Canton was being built in part with funds furnished by him, and a railway syndicate, for the purpose of constructing a line of railway from the big city of Canton to his own native town, was under process of formation, with the name of Spring Fragrance at its head.

No wonder then that Mr. Spring Fragrance muttered "Humph!" when Mrs. Spring Fragrance dilated upon the "divine right of learning," and that he should feel irritated and humiliated, when, after explaining to her his grievances, she should quote in the words of Confucius: "Be not concerned that men do not know you; be only concerned that you do not know them." And he had expected wifely sympathy.

He was about to leave the room in a somewhat chilled state of mind when she surprised him again by pattering across to him and following up a low curtsy with these words:

"I bow to you as the grass bends to the wind. Allow me to detain you for just one moment."

Mr. Spring Fragrance eyed her for a moment with suspicion.

"As I have told you, O Great Man," continued Mrs. Spring Fragrance, "I desire to write an immortal book, and now that I have learned from you that it is not necessary to acquire the 'divine right of learning' in order to accomplish things, I will begin the work without delay. My first subject will be 'The Inferior Woman of America.' Please advise me how I shall best inform myself concerning her."

Mr. Spring Fragrance, perceiving that his wife was now serious, and being easily mollified, sat himself down and rubbed his head. After thinking for a few moments he replied:

"It is the way in America, when a person is to be illustrated, for the illustrator to interview the person's friends. Perhaps, my dear, you had better confer with the Superior Woman."

"Surely," cried Mrs. Spring Fragrance, "no sage was ever so wise as my Great Man."

"But I lack the 'divine right of learning,'" dryly deplored Mr. Spring Fragrance.

"I am happy to hear it," answered Mrs. Spring Fragrance. "If you were a scholar you would have no time to read American poetry and American newspapers."

Mr. Spring Fragrance laughed heartily.

"You are no Chinese woman," he teased. "You are an American."

"Please bring me my parasol and my folding fan," said Mrs. Spring Fragrance. "I am going out for a walk."

And Mr. Spring Fragrance obeyed her.

IV

"This is from Mary Carman, who is in Portland," said the mother of the Superior Woman, looking up from the reading of a letter, as her daughter came in from the garden.

"Indeed," carelessly responded Miss Evebrook.

"Yes, it's chiefly about Will."

"Oh, is it? Well, read it then, dear. I'm interested in Will Carman, because of Alice Winthrop."

"I had hoped, Ethel, at one time that you would have been interested in him for his own sake. However, this is what she writes:

> "*I came here chiefly to rid myself of a melancholy mood which has taken possession of me lately, and also because I cannot bear to see my boy so changed toward me, owing to his infatuation for Alice Winthrop. It is incomprehensible to me how a son of mine can find any pleasure whatever in the society of such a girl. I have traced her history, and find that she is not only uneducated in the ordinary sense, but her environment, from childhood up, has been the sordid and demoralizing one of extreme poverty and ignorance. This girl, Alice, entered a law office at the age of fourteen, supposedly to do the work of an office boy. Now, after seven years in business, through the friendship and influence of men far above her socially, she holds the position of private secretary to the most influential man in Washington—a position which by rights belongs only to a well-educated young woman of good family. Many such applied. I myself sought to have Jane Walker appointed. Is it not disheartening to our woman's cause to be compelled to realize that girls such as this one can win men over to be their friends and lovers, when there are so many splendid young women who have been carefully trained to be companions and comrades of educated men?*"

"Pardon me, mother," interrupted Miss Evebrook, "but I have heard enough. Mrs. Carman is your friend and a well-meaning woman sometimes; but a woman suffragist, in the true sense, she certainly is not. Mark my words: If any young man had accomplished for himself what Alice Winthrop has accomplished, Mrs. Carman could not have said enough in his praise. It is women such as Alice Winthrop who, in spite of every drawback, have raised themselves to the level of those who have had every advantage, who are the pride and glory of America. There are thousands of them, all over this land: women who have been of service to others all their years and who have graduated from the university of life with honor. Women such as I, who are called the Superior Women of America, are after all nothing but schoolgirls in comparison."

Mrs. Evebrook eyed her daughter mutinously. "I don't see why you should feel like that," said she. "Alice is a dear bright child, and it is prejudice engendered by Mary Carman's disappointment about you and Will which is the real cause of poor Mary's bitterness toward her; but to my mind, Alice does not compare with my daughter. She would be frightened to death if she had to make a speech."

"You foolish mother!" rallied Miss Evebrook. "To stand upon a platform at woman suffrage meetings and exploit myself is certainly a great recompense to you and father for all the sacrifices you have made on my behalf. But since it pleases you, I do it with pleasure even on the nights when my beau should 'come a courting.' "

"There is many a one who would like to come, Ethel. You're the handsomest girl in this western town—and you know it."

"Stop that, mother. You know very well I have set my mind upon having ten years' freedom; ten years in which to love, live, suffer, see the world, and learn about men (not schoolboys) before I choose one."

"Alice Winthrop is the same age as you are, and looks like a child beside you."

"Physically, maybe; but her heart and mind are better developed. She has been out in the world all her life, I only a few months."

"Your lecture last week on 'The Opposite Sex' was splendid."

"Of course. I have studied one hundred books on the subject and attended fifty lectures. All that was necessary was to repeat in an original manner what was not by any means original."

Miss Evebrook went over to a desk and took a paper therefrom.

"This," said she, "is what Alice has written me in reply to my note suggesting that she attend next week the suffrage meeting, and give some of the experiences of her business career. The object I had in view when I requested the relation of her experiences was to use them as illustrations of the suppression and oppression of women by men. Strange to say, Alice and I have never conversed on this particular subject. If we had I would not have made this request of her, nor written her as I did. Listen:

"I should dearly love to please you, but I am afraid that my experiences, if related, would not help the cause. It may be, as you say, that men prevent women from rising to their level; but if there are such men, I have not met them. Ever since, when a little girl, I walked into a law office and asked for work, and the senior member kindly looked me over through his spectacles and inquired if I thought I could learn to index books, and the junior member glanced under my hat and said: "This is a pretty little girl and we must be pretty to her," I have loved and respected the men amongst whom I have worked and wherever I have worked. I may have been exceptionally fortunate, but I know this: the men for whom I have worked and amongst whom I have spent my life, whether they have been business or professional men, students or great lawyers and politicians, all alike have upheld me, inspired me, advised me, taught me, given me a broad outlook upon life for a woman; interested me in themselves and in their work. As to corrupting my mind and my morals, as you say so many men do, when they have young and innocent girls to deal with: As a woman, I look back over my years spent amongst business and professional men, and see myself, as I was at first, an impressionable, ignorant little girl, born a Bohemian, easy to lead and easy to win, but borne aloft and morally supported by the goodness of my brother men, the men amongst whom I worked. That is why, dear Ethel, you will have to forgive me, because I cannot carry out your design, and help your work, as otherwise I would like to do.'

"That, mother," declared Miss Evebrook, "answers all Mrs. Carman's insinuations, and should make her ashamed of herself. Can anyone know the sentiments which little Alice entertains toward men, and wonder at her winning out as she has?"

Mrs. Evebrook was about to make reply, when her glance happening to stray out of the window, she noticed a pink parasol.

"Mrs. Spring Fragrance!" she ejaculated, while her daughter went to the door and invited in the owner of the pink parasol, who was seated in a veranda rocker calmly writing in a notebook.

"I'm so sorry that we did not hear your ring, Mrs. Spring Fragrance," said she.

"There is no necessity for you to sorrow," replied the little Chinese woman. "I did not expect you to hear a ring which rang not. I failed to pull the bell."

"You forgot, I suppose," suggested Ethel Evebrook.

"Is it wise to tell secrets?" ingenuously inquired Mrs. Spring Fragrance.

"Yes, to your friends. Oh, Mrs. Spring Fragrance, you are *so* refreshing."

"I have pleasure, then, in confiding to you. I have an ambition to accomplish an immortal book about the Americans, and the conversation I heard through the window was so interesting to me that I thought I would take some of it down for my book before I intruded myself. With your kind permission I will translate for your correction."

"I shall be delighted—honored," said Miss Evebrook, her cheeks glowing and her laugh rippling, "if you will promise me that you will also translate for our friend, Mrs. Carman."

"Ah, yes, poor Mrs. Carman! My heart is so sad for her," murmured the little Chinese woman.

V

When the mother of Will Carman returned from Portland, the first person upon whom she called was Mrs. Spring Fragrance. Having lived in China while her late husband was in the customs service there, Mrs. Carman's prejudices did not extend to the Chinese, and ever since the Spring Fragrances had become the occupants of the villa beside the Carmans', there had been social good feeling between the American and Chinese families. Indeed, Mrs. Carman was wont to declare that amongst all her acquaintants there was not one more congenial and interesting than little Mrs. Spring Fragrance. So after she had sipped a cup of delicious tea, tasted some piquant candied limes, and told Mrs. Spring Fragrance all about her visit to the Oregon city and the Chinese people she had met there, she reverted to a personal trouble confided to Mrs. Spring Fragrance some months before and dwelt upon it for more than half an hour. Then she checked herself and gazed at Mrs. Spring Fragrance in surprise. Hitherto she had found the little Chinese woman sympathetic and consoling. Chinese ideas of filial duty chimed in with her own. But today Mrs. Spring Fragrance seemed strangely uninterested and unresponsive.

"Perhaps," gently suggested the American woman, who was nothing if not sensitive, "you have some trouble yourself. If so, my dear, tell me all about it."

"Oh, no!" answered Mrs. Spring Fragrance brightly. "I have no troubles to tell; but all the while I am thinking about the book I am writing."

"A book!"

"Yes, a book about Americans, an immortal book."

"My dear Mrs. Spring Fragrance!" exclaimed her visitor in amazement.

"The American woman writes books about the Chinese. Why not a Chinese woman write books about the Americans?"

"I see what you mean. Why, yes, of course. What an original idea!"

"Yes, I think that is what it is. My book I shall take from the words of others."

"What do you mean, my dear?"

"I listen to what is said, I apprehend, I write it down. Let me illustrate by the 'Inferior Woman' subject. The Inferior Woman is most interesting to me because you have told me that your son is much in love with her. My husband advised me to learn about the Inferior Woman from the Superior Woman. I go to see the Superior Woman. I sit on the veranda of the Superior Woman's house. I listen to her converse with her mother about the Inferior Woman. With the speed of flames I write down all I hear. When I enter the house the Superior Woman advises me that what I write is correct. May I read to you?"

"I shall be pleased to hear what you have written; but I do not think you were wise in your choice of subject," returned Mrs. Carman somewhat primly.

"I am sorry I am not wise. Perhaps I had better not read?" said Mrs. Spring Fragrance with humility.

"Yes, yes, do, please."

There was eagerness in Mrs. Carman's voice. What could Ethel Evebrook have to say about that girl!

When Mrs. Spring Fragrance had finished reading, she looked up into the face of her American friend—a face in which there was nothing now but tenderness.

"Mrs. Mary Carman," said she, "you are so good as to admire my husband because he is what the Americans call 'a man who has made himself.' Why then do you not admire the Inferior Woman who is a woman who has made herself?"

"I think I do," said Mrs. Carman slowly.

VI

It was an evening that invited reverie. The far stretches of the sea were gray with mist, and the city itself, lying around the sweep of the bay, seemed dusky and distant. From her cottage window Alice Winthrop looked silently at the open world around her. It seemed a long time since she had heard Will Carman's whistle. She wondered if he were still angry with her. She was sorry that he had left her in anger, and yet not sorry. If she had not made him believe that she was proud and selfish, the parting would have been much harder; and perhaps had he known the truth and realized that it was for his sake, and not for her own, that she was sending him away from her, he might have refused to leave her at all. His was such an imperious nature. And then they would have married—right away. Alice caught her breath a little, and then she sighed. But they would not have been happy. No, that could not have been possible if his mother did not like her. When a gulf of prejudice lies between the wife and mother of a man, that man's life is not what it should be. And even supposing she and Will could have lost themselves in each other, and been able to imagine themselves perfectly satisfied with life together, would it have been right? The question of right and wrong was a very real one to Alice Winthrop. She put herself in the place of the mother of her lover—a lonely elderly woman, a widow with an only son, upon whom she had expended all her love and care ever since, in her early youth, she had been bereaved of his father. What anguish of heart would be hers if that son deserted her for one whom she, his mother, deemed unworthy! Prejudices are prejudices. They are like diseases.

The poor, pale, elderly woman, who cherished bitter and resentful feelings toward the girl whom her son loved, was more an object of pity than condemnation to the girl herself.

She lifted her eyes to the undulating line of hills beyond the water. From behind them came a silver light. "Yes," said she aloud to herself—and, though she knew it not, there was an infinite pathos in such philosophy from one so young—"if life cannot be bright and beautiful for me, at least it can be peaceful and contented."

The light behind the hills died away; darkness crept over the sea. Alice withdrew from the window and went and knelt before the open fire in her sitting room. Her cottage companion, the young woman who rented the place with her, had not yet returned from town.

Alice did not turn on the light. She was seeing pictures in the fire, and in every picture was the same face and form—the face and form of a fine, handsome young man with love and hope in his eyes. No, not always love and hope. In the last picture of all there was an expression which she wished she could forget. And yet she would remember—ever—always—and with it, these words: "Is it nothing to you—nothing—to tell a man that you love him, and then to bid him go?"

Yes, but when she had told him she loved him she had not dreamed that her love for him and his for her would estrange him from one who, before ever she had come to this world, had pillowed his head on her breast.

Suddenly this girl, so practical, so humorous, so clever in everyday life, covered her face with her hands and sobbed like a child. Two roads of life had lain before her and she had chosen the hardest.

The warning bell of an automobile passing the crossroads checked her tears. That reminded her that Nellie Blake would soon be home. She turned on the light and went to the bedroom and bathed her eyes. Nellie must have forgotten her key. There she was knocking.

—

The chill sea air was sweet with the scent of roses as Mary Carman stood upon the threshold of the little cottage, and beheld in the illumination from within the young girl whom she had called "the Inferior Woman."

"I have come, Miss Winthrop," said she, "to beg of you to return home with me. Will, reckless boy, met with a slight accident while out shooting, so could not come for you himself. He has told me that he loves you, and if you love him, I want to arrange for the prettiest wedding of the season. Come, dear!"

"I am so glad," said Mrs. Spring Fragrance, "that Will Carman's bird is in his nest and his felicity is assured."

"What about the Superior Woman?" asked Mr. Spring Fragrance.

"Ah, the Superior Woman! Radiantly beautiful, and gifted with the divine right of learning! I love well the Inferior Woman; but, O Great Man, when we have a daughter, may Heaven ordain that she walk in the groove of the Superior Woman."

THE WISDOM OF THE NEW

I

Old Li Wang, the peddler, who had lived in the land beyond the sea, was wont to declare: "For every cent that a man makes here, he can make one hundred there."

"Then, why," would ask Sankwei, "do you now have to move from door to door to fill your bowl with rice?"

And the old man would sigh and answer:

"Because where one learns how to make gold, one also learns how to lose it."

"How to lose it!" echoed Wou Sankwei. "Tell me all about it."

So the old man would tell stories about the winning and the losing, and the stories of the losing were even more fascinating than the stories of the winning.

"Yes, that was life," he would conclude. "Life, life."

At such times the boy would gaze across the water with wistful eyes. The land beyond the sea was calling to him.

The place was a sleepy little south coast town where the years slipped by monotonously. The boy was the only son of the man, who had been the town magistrate.

Had his father lived, Wou Sankwei would have been sent to complete his schooling in another province. As it was he did nothing but sleep, dream, and occasionally get into mischief. What else was there to do? His mother and sister waited upon him hand and foot. Was he not the son of the house? The family income was small, scarcely sufficient for their needs; but there was no way by which he could add to it, unless, indeed, he disgraced the name of Wou by becoming a common fisherman. The great green waves lifted white arms of foam to him, and the fishes gleaming and lurking in the waters seemed to beseech him to draw them from the deep; but his mother shook her head.

"Should you become a fisherman," said she, "your family would lose face. Remember that your father was a magistrate."

When he was about nineteen there returned to the town one who had been absent for many years. Ching Kee, like old Li Wang, had also lived in the land beyond the sea; but unlike old Li Wang he had accumulated a small fortune.

" 'Tis a hard life over there," said he, "but 'tis worthwhile. At least one can be a man, and can work at what work comes his way without losing face." Then he laughed at Wou Sankwei's flabby muscles, at his soft, dark eyes, and plump, white hands.

"If you lived in America," said he, "you would learn to be ashamed of such beauty."

Whereupon Wou Sankwei made up his mind that he would go to America, the land beyond the sea. Better any life than that of a woman-man.

He talked long and earnestly with his mother. "Give me your blessing," said he. "I will work and save money. What I send home will bring you many a comfort, and when I come back to China, it may be that I shall be able to complete my studies and obtain a degree. If not, my knowledge of the foreign language which I shall acquire, will enable me to take a position which will not disgrace the name of Wou."

His mother listened and thought. She was ambitious for her son, whom she loved beyond all things on earth. Moreover, had not Sik Ping, a Canton merchant who had visited the little town two moons ago, declared to Hum Wah, who traded in palm leaves, that the signs of the times were that the son of a cobbler, returned from America with the foreign language, could easier command a position of consequence than the son of a schoolteacher unacquainted with any tongue but that of his motherland?

"Very well," she acquiesced; "but before you go I must find you a wife. Only your son, my son, can comfort me for your loss."

II

Wou Sankwei stood behind his desk, busily entering figures in a long yellow book. Now and then he would thrust the hair pencil with which he worked behind his ears and manipulate with deft fingers a Chinese counting machine. Wou Sankwei was the junior partner and bookkeeper of the firm of Leung Tang Wou & Co. of San Francisco. He had been in America seven years and had made good use of his time. Self-improvement had been his object and ambition, even more than the acquirement of a fortune, and who, looking at his fine, intelligent face and listening to his careful English, could say that he had failed?

One of his partners called his name. Some ladies wished to speak to him. Wou Sankwei hastened to the front of the store. One of his callers, a motherly looking woman, was the friend who had taken him under her wing shortly after his arrival in America. She had come to invite him to spend the evening with her and her niece, the young girl who accompanied her.

After his callers had left, Sankwei returned to his desk and worked steadily until the hour for his evening meal, which he took in the Chinese restaurant across the street from the bazaar. He hurried through with this, as before going to his friend's house, he had a somewhat important letter to write and mail. His mother had died a year before, and his uncle, to whom he was writing, had taken his wife and son into his home until such time as his nephew could send for them. Now the time had come.

Wou Sankwei's memory of the woman who was his wife was very faint. How could it be otherwise? She had come to him but three weeks before the sailing of the vessel which had brought him to America, and until then he had not seen her face. But she was his wife and the mother of his son. Ever since he had worked in America he had sent money for her support, and she had proved a good daughter to his mother.

As he sat down to write he decided that he would welcome her with a big dinner to his countrymen.

"Yes," he replied to Mrs. Dean, later on in the evening, "I have sent for my wife."

"I am so glad," said the lady. "Mr. Wou"—turning to her niece—"has not seen his wife for seven years."

"Deary me!" exclaimed the young girl. "What a lot of letters you must have written!"

"I have not written her one," returned the young man somewhat stiffly.

Adah Charlton looked up in surprise. "Why—" she began.

"Mr. Wou used to be such a studious boy when I first knew him," interrupted Mrs. Dean, laying her hand affectionately upon the young man's shoulder. "Now, it is all business. But you won't forget the concert on Saturday evening."

"No, I will not forget," answered Wou Sankwei.

"He has never written to his wife," explained Mrs. Dean when she and her niece were alone, "because his wife can neither read nor write."

"Oh, isn't that sad!" murmured Adah Charlton, her own winsome face becoming pensive.

"They don't seem to think so. It is the Chinese custom to educate only the boys. At least it has been so in the past. Sankwei himself is unusually bright. Poor boy! He began life here as a laundryman, and you may be sure that it must have been hard on him, for, as the son of a petty Chinese Government official, he had not been accustomed to manual labor. But Chinese character is wonderful; and now after seven years in this country, he enjoys a reputation as a businessman amongst his countrymen, and is as up to date as any young American."

"But, Auntie, isn't it dreadful to think that a man should live away from his wife for so many years without any communication between them whatsoever except through others."

"It is dreadful to our minds, but not to theirs. Everything with them is a matter of duty. Sankwei married his wife as a matter of duty. He sends for her as a matter of duty."

"I wonder if it is all duty on her side," mused the girl.

Mrs. Dean smiled. "You are too romantic, Adah," said she. "I hope, however, that when she does come, they will be happy together. I think almost as much of Sankwei as I do of my own boy."

III

Pau Lin, the wife of Wou Sankwei, sat in a corner of the deck of the big steamer, awaiting the coming of her husband. Beside her, leaning his little queued head against her shoulder, stood her six-year-old son. He had been ailing throughout the voyage, and his small face was pinched with pain. His mother, who had been nursing him every night since the ship had left port, appeared very worn and tired. This, despite the fact that with a feminine desire to make herself fair to see in the eyes of her husband, she had arrayed herself in a heavily embroidered purple costume, whitened her forehead and cheeks with powder, and tinted her lips with carmine.

He came at last, looking over and beyond her. There were two others of her countrywomen awaiting the men who had sent for them, and each had a child, so that for a moment he seemed somewhat bewildered. Only when the ship's officer pointed out and named her, did he know her as his. Then he came forward, spoke a few words of formal welcome, and, lifting the child in his arms, began questioning her as to its health.

She answered in low monosyllables. At his greeting she had raised her patient eyes to his face—the face of the husband whom she had not seen for seven long years—then the eager look of expectancy which had crossed her own faded away, her eyelids drooped, and her countenance assumed an almost sullen expression.

"Ah, poor Sankwei!" exclaimed Mrs. Dean, who with Adah Charlton stood some little distance apart from the family group.

"Poor wife!" murmured the young girl. She moved forward and would have taken in her own white hands the ringed ones of the Chinese woman, but the young man gently restrained her. "She cannot understand you," said he. As the young girl fell back, he explained to his wife the presence of the stranger women. They were there to bid her welcome; they were kind and good and wished to be her friends as well as his.

Pau Lin looked away. Adah Charlton's bright face, and the tone in her husband's voice when he spoke to the young girl, aroused a suspicion in her mind—a suspicion natural to one who had come from a land where friendship between a man and woman is almost unknown.

"Poor little thing! How shy she is!" exclaimed Mrs. Dean.

Sankwei was glad that neither she nor the young girl understood the meaning of the averted face.

Thus began Wou Sankwei's life in America as a family man. He soon became accustomed to the change, which was not such a great one after all. Pau Lin was more of an accessory than a part of his life. She interfered not at all with his studies, his business, or his friends, and when not engaged in housework or sewing, spent most of her time in the society of one or the other of the merchants' wives who lived in the flats and apartments around her own. She kept up the Chinese custom of taking her meals after her husband or at a separate table, and observed faithfully the rule laid down for her by her late mother-in-law: to keep a quiet tongue in the presence of her man. Sankwei, on his part, was always kind and indulgent. He bought her silk dresses, hair ornaments, fans, and sweetmeats. He ordered her favorite dishes from the Chinese restaurant. When she wished to go out with her women friends, he hired a carriage, and shortly after her advent erected behind her sleeping room a chapel for the ancestral tablet and gorgeous goddess which she had brought overseas with her.

Upon the child both parents lavished affection. He was a quaint, serious little fellow, small for his age and requiring much care. Although naturally much attached to his mother, he became also very fond of his father, who, more like an elder brother than a parent, delighted in playing all kinds of games with him, and whom he followed about like a little dog. Adah Charlton took a great fancy to him and sketched him in many different poses for a book on Chinese children which she was illustrating.

"He will be strong enough to go to school next year," said Sankwei to her one day. "Later on I intend to put him through an American college."

"What does your wife think of a Western training for him?" inquired the young girl.

"I have not consulted her about the matter," he answered. "A woman does not understand such things."

"A woman, Mr. Wou," declared Adah, "understands such things as well as and sometimes better than a man."

"An American woman, maybe," amended Sankwei; "but not a Chinese."

From the first, Pau Lin had shown no disposition to become Americanized, and Sankwei himself had not urged it.

"I do appreciate the advantages of becoming Westernized," said he to Mrs. Dean, whose influence and interest in his studies in America had helped him to become what he was, "but it is not as if she had come here as I came, in her learning days. The time for learning with her is over."

One evening, upon returning from his store, he found the little Yen sobbing pitifully.

"What!" he teased. "A man—and weeping."

The boy tried to hide his face, and as he did so, the father noticed that his little hand was red and swollen. He strode into the kitchen where Pau Lin was preparing the evening meal.

"The little child who is not strong—is there anything he could do to merit the infliction of pain?" he questioned.

Pau Lin faced her husband. "Yes, I think so," said she.

"What?"

"I forbade him to speak the language of the white women, and he disobeyed me. He had words in that tongue with the white boy from the next street."

Sankwei was astounded.

"We are living in the white man's country," said he. "The child will have to learn the white man's language."

"Not my child," answered Pau Lin.

Sankwei turned away from her. "Come, little one," said he to his son, "we will take supper tonight at the restaurant, and afterward Yen shall see a show."

Pau Lin laid down the dish of vegetables which she was straining and took from a hook a small wrap which she adjusted around the boy.

"Now go with thy father," said she sternly.

But the boy clung to her—to the hand which had punished him. "I will sup with you," he cried, "I will sup with you."

"Go," repeated his mother, pushing him from her. And as the two passed over the threshold, she called to the father: "Keep the wrap around the child. The night air is chill."

Late that night, while father and son were peacefully sleeping, the wife and mother arose, and lifting gently the unconscious boy, bore him into the next room where she sat down with him in a rocker. Waking, he clasped his arms around her neck. Backward and forward she rocked him, passionately caressing the wounded hand and crooning and crying until he fell asleep again.

The first chastisement that the son of Wou Sankwei had received from his mother was because he had striven to follow in the footsteps of his father and use the language of the stranger.

"You did perfectly right," said old Sien Tau the following morning, as she leaned over her balcony to speak to the wife of Wou Sankwei. "Had I again a son to rear, I should see to it that he followed not after the white people."

Sien Tau's son had married a white woman, and his children passed their grandame on the street without recognition.

"In this country, she is most happy who has no child," said Lae Choo, resting her elbow upon the shoulder of Sien Tau. "A Toy, the young daughter of Lew Wing, is as bold and free in her ways as are the white women, and her name is on all the men's tongues. What prudent man of our race would take her as wife?"

"One needs not to be born here to be made a fool of," joined in Pau Lin, appearing at another balcony door. "Think of Hum Wah. From sunrise till midnight he worked for fourteen years, then a white man came along and persuaded from him every dollar, promising to return doublefold within the moon. Many moons have risen and waned, and Hum Wah still waits on this side of the sea for the white man and his money. Meanwhile, his father and mother, who looked long for his coming, have passed beyond returning."

"The new religion—what trouble it brings!" exclaimed Lae Choo. "My man received word yestereve that the good old mother of Chee Ping—he who was baptized a Christian at the last baptizing in the Mission around the corner—had her head secretly severed from her body by the steadfast people of the village, as soon as the news reached there. 'Twas the first violent death in the records of the place. This happened to the mother of one of the boys attending the Mission corner of my street."

"No doubt, the poor old mother, having lost face, minded not so much the losing of her head," sighed Pau Lin. She gazed below her curiously. The American Chinatown held a strange fascination for the girl from the seacoast village. Streaming along the street was a motley throng made up of all nationalities. The singsong voices of girls whom respectable merchants' wives shudder to name, were calling to one another from high balconies up shadowy alleys. A fat barber was laughing hilariously at a drunken white man who had fallen into a gutter; a withered old fellow, carrying a bird in a cage, stood at the corner entreating passersby to have a good fortune told; some children were burning punk on the curbstone. There went by a stalwart Chief of the Six Companies engaged in earnest confab with a yellow-robed priest from the joss house. A Chinese dressed in the latest American style and a very blond woman, laughing immoderately, were entering a Chinese restaurant together. Above all the hubbub of voices was heard the clang of electric cars and the jarring of heavy wheels over cobblestones.

Pau Lin raised her head and looked her thoughts at the old woman, Sien Tau.

"Yes," nodded the dame, "'tis a mad place in which to bring up a child."

Pau Lin went back into the house, gave little Yen his noonday meal, and dressed him with care. His father was to take him out that afternoon. She questioned the boy, as she braided his queue, concerning the white women whom he visited with his father.

It was evening when they returned—Wou Sankwei and his boy. The little fellow ran up to her in high glee. "See, Mother," said he, pulling off his cap, "I am like father now. I wear no queue."

The mother looked down upon him—at the little round head from which the queue, which had been her pride, no longer dangled.

"Ah!" she cried. "I am ashamed of you; I am ashamed!"

The boy stared at her, hurt and disappointed.

"Never mind, son," comforted his father. "It is all right."

Pau Lin placed the bowls of seaweed and chickens' liver before them and went back to the kitchen where her own meal was waiting. But she did not eat. She was saying within herself: "It is for the white woman he has done this; it is for the white woman!"

Later, as she laid the queue of her son within the trunk wherein lay that of his father, long since cast aside, she discovered a picture of Mrs. Dean, taken when the American woman had first become the teacher and benefactress of the youthful laundryman. She ran over with it to her husband. "Here," said she; "it is a picture of one of your white friends." Sankwei took it from her almost reverently, "That woman," he explained, "has been to me as a mother."

"And the young woman—the one with eyes the color of blue china—is she also as a mother?" inquired Pau Lin gently.

But for all her gentleness, Wou Sankwei flushed angrily.

"Never speak of her," he cried. "Never speak of her!"

"Ha, ha, ha! Ha, ha, ha!" laughed Pau Lin. It was a soft and not unmelodious laugh, but to Wou Sankwei it sounded almost sacrilegious.

Nevertheless, he soon calmed down. Pau Lin was his wife, and to be kind to her was not only his duty but his nature. So when his little boy climbed into his lap and besought his father to pipe him a tune, he reached for his flute and called to Pau Lin to put aside work for that night. He would play her some Chinese music. And Pau Lin, whose heart and mind, undiverted by change, had been concentrated upon Wou Sankwei ever since the day she had become his wife, smothered for the time being the bitterness in her heart, and succumbed to the magic of her husband's playing—a magic which transported her in thought to the old Chinese days, the old Chinese days whose impression and influence ever remain with the exiled sons and daughters of China.

IV

That a man should take to himself two wives, or even three, if he thought proper, seemed natural and right in the eyes of Wou Pau Lin. She herself had come from a home where there were two broods of children and where her mother and her father's other wife had eaten their meals together as sisters. In that home there had not always been peace; but each woman, at least, had the satisfaction of knowing that her man did not regard or treat the other woman as her superior. To each had fallen the common lot—to bear children to the man, and the man was master of all.

But, oh! the humiliation and shame of bearing children to a man who looked up to another woman—and a woman of another race—as a being above the common uses of women. There is a jealousy of the mind more poignant than any mere animal jealousy.

When Wou Sankwei's second child was two weeks old, Adah Charlton and her aunt called to see the little one, and the young girl chatted brightly with the father and played merrily with Yen, who was growing strong and merry. The American women could not, of course, converse with the Chinese; but Adah placed beside her a bunch of beautiful flowers, pressed her hand, and looked down upon her with radiant eyes. Secure in the difference of race, in the love of many friends, and in the happiness of her chosen work, no suspicion whatever crossed her mind that the woman whose husband was her aunt's protégé tasted everything bitter because of her.

After the visitors had gone, Pau Lin, who had been watching

her husband's face while the young artist was in the room, said to him:

"She can be happy who takes all and gives nothing."

"Takes all and gives nothing," echoed her husband. "What do you mean?"

"She has taken all your heart," answered Pau Lin, "but she has not given you a son. It is I who have had that task."

"You are my wife," answered Wou Sankwei. "And she—oh! how can you speak of her so? She, who is as a pure water-flower—a lily!"

He went out of the room, carrying with him a little painting of their boy, which Adah Charlton had given to him as she bade him goodbye and which he had intended to show with pride to the mother.

It was on the day that the baby died that Pau Lin first saw the little picture. It had fallen out of her husband's coat pocket when he lifted the tiny form in his arms and declared it lifeless. Even in that first moment of loss Pau Lin, stooping to pick up the portrait, had shrunk back in horror, crying: "She would cast a spell! She would cast a spell!"

She set her heel upon the face of the picture and destroyed it beyond restoration.

"You know not what you say and do," sternly rebuked Sankwei. He would have added more, but the mystery of the dead child's look forbade him.

"The loss of a son is as the loss of a limb," said he to his childless partner, as under the red glare of the lanterns they sat discussing the sad event.

"But you are not without consolation," returned Leung Tsao. "Your firstborn grows in strength and beauty."

"True," assented Wou Sankwei, his heavy thoughts becoming lighter.

And Pau Lin, in her curtained balcony overhead, drew closer her child and passionately cried:

"Sooner would I, O heart of my heart, that the light of thine eyes were also quenched, than that thou shouldst be contaminated with the wisdom of the new."

V

The Chinese women friends of Wou Pau Lin gossiped among themselves, and their gossip reached the ears of the American woman friend of Pau Lin's husband. Since the days of her widowhood Mrs. Dean had devoted herself earnestly and wholeheartedly to the betterment of the condition and the uplifting of the young Chinese workingmen who came to America. Their appeal and need, as she had told her niece, was for closer acquaintance with the knowledge of the Western people, and *that* she had undertaken to give them, as far as she was able. The rewards and satisfactions of her work had been rich in some cases. Witness Wou Sankwei.

But the gossip had reached and much perturbed her. What was it that they said Wou Sankwei's wife had declared—that her little son should not go to an American school nor learn the American learning. Such bigotry and narrow-mindedness! How sad to think of! Here was a man who had benefited and profited by living in America, anxious to have his son receive the benefits of a Western education—and here was this man's wife opposing him with her ignorance and hampering him with her unreasonable jealousy.

Yes, she had heard that too. That Wou Sankwei's wife was jealous—jealous—and her husband the most moral of men, the kindest and the most generous.

"Of what is she jealous?" she questioned Adah Charlton. "Other Chinese men's wives, I have known, have had cause to be jealous, for it is true some of them are dreadfully immoral and openly support two or more wives. But not Wou Sankwei. And this little Pau Lin. She has everything that a Chinese woman could wish for."

A sudden flash of intuition came to the girl, rendering her for a moment speechless. When she did find words, she said:

"Everything that a Chinese woman could wish for, you say. Auntie, I do not believe there is any real difference between the feelings of a Chinese wife and an American wife. Sankwei is treating Pau Lin as he would treat her were he living in China. Yet it cannot be the same to her as if she were in their own country, where he would not come in contact with American women. A woman is a woman with intuitions and perceptions, whether Chinese or American, whether educated or uneducated, and Sankwei's wife must have noticed, even on the day of her arrival, her husband's manner toward us, and contrasted it with his manner toward her. I did not realize this before you told me that she was jealous. I only wish I had. Now, for all her ignorance, I can see that the poor little thing became more of an American in that one half hour on the steamer than Wou Sankwei, for all your pride in him, has become in seven years."

Mrs. Dean rested her head on her hand. She was evidently much perplexed.

"What you say may be, Adah," she replied after a while; "but even so, it is Sankwei whom I have known so long, who has my sympathies. He has much to put up with. They have drifted seven years of life apart. There is no bond of interest or sympathy between them, save the boy. Yet never the slightest hint of trouble has come to me from his own lips. Before the coming of Pau Lin, he would confide in me every little thing that worried him, as if he were my own son. Now he maintains absolute silence as to his private affairs."

"Chinese principles," observed Adah, resuming her work. "Yes, I admit Sankwei has some puzzles to solve. Naturally, when he tries to live two lives—that of a Chinese and that of an American."

"He is compelled to that," retorted Mrs. Dean. "Is it not what we teach these Chinese boys—to become Americans? And yet, they are Chinese, and must, in a sense, remain so."

Adah did not answer.

Mrs. Dean sighed. "Poor, dear children, both of them," mused she. "I feel very low-spirited over the matter. I suppose you wouldn't care to come downtown with me. I should like to have another chat with Mrs. Wing Sing."

"I shall be glad of the change," replied Adah, laying down her brushes.

Rows of lanterns suspended from many balconies shed a mellow, moonshiny radiance. On the walls and doors were splashes of red paper inscribed with characters. In the narrow streets, booths decorated with flowers, and banners and screens painted with immense figures of josses diverted the eye; while bands of musicians in gaudy silks shrilled and banged, piped and fluted.

Everybody seemed to be out of doors—men, women, and children—and nearly all were in holiday attire. A couple of priests, in vivid scarlet and yellow robes, were kowtowing before an altar covered with a rich cloth, embroidered in white and silver. Some Chinese students from the University of California stood looking on with comprehending, half-scornful interest; three girls lavishly dressed in colored silks, with their black hair plastered back from their faces and heavily bejeweled behind, chirped and chattered in a gilded balcony above them like birds in a cage. Little children, their hands full of half-moon-shaped cakes, were pattering about, with eyes, for all the hour, as bright as stars.

Chinatown was celebrating the Harvest Moon Festival, and Adah Charlton was glad that she had an opportunity to see something of the celebration before she returned East. Mrs. Dean, familiar with the Chinese people and the mazes of Chinatown, led her around fearlessly, pointing out this and that object of interest and explaining to her its meaning. Seeing that it was a gala night, she had abandoned her idea of calling upon the Chinese friend.

Just as they turned a corner leading up to the street where Wou Sankwei's place of business and residence was situated, a pair of little hands grasped Mrs. Dean's skirt and a delighted little voice piped: "See me! See me!" It was little Yen, resplendent in mauve-colored pantaloons and embroidered vest and cap. Behind him was a tall man whom both women recognized.

"How do you happen to have Yen with you?" Adah asked.

"His father handed him over to me as a sort of guide, counsellor, and friend. The little fellow is very amusing."

"See over here," interrupted Yen. He hopped over the alley to where the priests stood by the altar. The grown people followed him.

"What is that man chanting?" asked Adah. One of the priests had mounted a table, and with arms outstretched toward the moon sailing high in the heavens, seemed to be making some sort of an invocation.

Her friend listened for some moments before replying:

"It is a sort of apotheosis of the moon. I have heard it on a like occasion in Hankow, and the Chinese *bonze* who officiated gave me a translation. I almost know it by heart. May I repeat it to you?"

Mrs. Dean and Yen were examining the screen with the big josses.

"Yes, I should like to hear it," said Adah.

"Then fix your eyes upon Diana."

"Dear and lovely moon, as I watch thee pursuing thy solitary course o'er the silent heavens, heart-easing thoughts steal o'er me and calm my passionate soul. Thou art so sweet, so serious, so serene, that thou causest me to forget the stormy emotions which crash like jarring discords across the harmony of life, and bringest to my memory a voice scarce ever heard amidst the warring of the world—love's low voice.

"Thou art so peaceful and so pure that it seemeth as if naught false or ignoble could dwell beneath thy gentle radiance, and that earnestness—even the earnestness of genius—must glow within the bosom of him on whose head thy beams fall like blessings.

"The magic of thy sympathy disburtheneth me of many sorrows, and thoughts, which, like the songs of the sweetest sylvan singer, are too dear and sacred for the careless ears of day, gush forth with unconscious eloquence when thou art the only listener.

"Dear and lovely moon, there are some who say that those who dwell in the sunlit fields of reason should fear to wander through the moonlit valleys of imagination; but I, who have ever been a pilgrim and a stranger in the realm of the wise, offer to thee the homage of a heart which appreciates that thou graciously shinest—even on the fool."

"Is that really Chinese?" queried Adah.

"No doubt about it—in the main. Of course, I cannot swear to it word for word."

"I should think that there would be some reference to the fruits of the earth—the harvest. I always understood that the Chinese religion was so practical."

"Confucianism is. But the Chinese mind requires two religions. Even the most commonplace Chinese has yearnings for something above everyday life. Therefore, he combines with his Confucianism, Buddhism—or, in this country, Christianity."

"Thank you for the information. It has given me a key to the mind of a certain Chinese in whom Auntie and I are interested."

"And who is this particular Chinese in whom you are interested."

"The father of the little boy who is with us tonight."

"Wou Sankwei! Why, here he comes with Lee Tong Hay. Are you acquainted with Lee Tong Hay?"

"No, but I believe Aunt is. Plays and sings in vaudeville, doesn't he?"

"Yes; he can turn himself into a German, a Scotchman, an Irishman, or an American, with the greatest ease, and is as natural in each character as he is as a Chinaman. Hello, Lee Tong Hay."

"Hello, Mr. Stimson."

While her friend was talking to the lively young Chinese who had answered his greeting, Adah went over to where Wou Sankwei stood speaking to Mrs. Dean.

"Yen begins school next week," said her aunt, drawing her arm within her own. It was time to go home.

Adah made no reply. She was settling her mind to do something quite out of the ordinary. Her aunt often called her romantic and impractical. Perhaps she was.

VI

"Auntie went out of town this morning," said Adah Charlton. "I phoned for you to come up, Sankwei, because I wished to have a personal and private talk with you."

"Any trouble, Miss Adah," inquired the young merchant. "Anything I can do for you?"

Mrs. Dean often called upon him to transact little business matters for her or to consult with him on various phases of her social and family life.

"I don't know what I would do without Sankwei's head to manage for me," she often said to her niece.

"No," replied the girl, "you do too much for us. You always have, ever since I've known you. It's a shame for us to have allowed you."

"What are you talking about, Miss Adah? Since I came to America your aunt has made this house like a home to me, and, of course, I take an interest in it and like to do anything for it that a man can. I am always happy when I come here."

"Yes, I know you are, poor old boy," said Adah to herself.

Aloud she said: "I have something to say to you which I would like you to hear. Will you listen, Sankwei?"

"Of course I will," he answered.

"Well then," went on Adah, "I asked you to come here today because I have heard that there is trouble at your house and that your wife is jealous of you."

"Would you please not talk about that, Miss Adah. It is a matter which you cannot understand."

"You promised to listen and heed. I do understand, even though I cannot speak to your wife nor find out what she feels and thinks. I know you, Sankwei, and I can see just how the trouble has arisen. As soon as I heard that your wife was jealous I knew why she was jealous."

"Why?" he queried.

"Because," she answered unflinchingly, "you are thinking far too much of other women."

"Too much of other women?" echoed Sankwei dazedly. "I did not know that."

"No, you didn't. That is why I am telling you. But you are, Sankwei. And you are becoming too Americanized. My aunt encourages you to become so, and she is a good woman, with the best and highest of motives; but we are all liable to make mistakes, and it is a mistake to try and make a Chinese man into an American—if he has a wife who is to remain as she always has been. It would be different if you were not married and were a man free to advance. But you are not."

"What am I to do then, Miss Adah? You say that I think too much of other women besides her, and that I am too much Americanized. What can I do about it now that it is so?"

"First of all you must think of your wife. She has done for you what no American woman would do—came to you to be your wife, love you, and serve you without even knowing you—took you on trust altogether. You must remember that for many years she was chained in a little cottage to care for your ailing and aged mother—a hard task indeed for a young girl. You must remember that you are the only man in the world to her, and that you have always been the only one that she has ever cared for. Think of her during all the years you are here, living a lonely hard-working life—a baby and an old woman her only companions. For this, she had left all her own relations. No American woman would have sacrificed herself so.

"And, now, what has she? Only you and her housework. The white woman reads, plays, paints, attends concerts, entertainments, lectures, absorbs herself in the work she likes, and in the course of her life thinks of and cares for a great many people. She has much to make her happy besides her husband. The Chinese woman has him only."

"And her boy."

"Yes, her boy," repeated Adah Charlton, smiling in spite of herself, but lapsing into seriousness the moment after. "There's another reason for you to drop the American for a time and go back to being a Chinese. For the sake of your darling little boy, you and your wife should live together kindly and cheerfully. That is much more important for his welfare than that he should go to the American school and become Americanized."

"It is my ambition to put him through both American and Chinese schools."

"But what he needs most of all is a loving mother."

"She loves him all right."

"Then why do you not love her as you should? If I were married I would not think my husband loved me very much if he preferred spending his evenings in the society of other women than in mine, and was so much more polite and deferential to other women than he was to me. Can't you understand now why your wife is jealous?"

Wou Sankwei stood up.

"Goodbye," said Adah Charlton, giving him her hand.

"Goodbye," said Wou Sankwei.

Had he been a white man, there is no doubt that Adah Charlton's little lecture would have had a contrary effect from what she meant it to have. At least, the lectured would have been somewhat cynical as to her sincerity. But Wou Sankwei was not a white man. He was a Chinese, and did not see any reason for insincerity in a matter as important as that which Adah Charlton had brought before him. He felt himself exiled from Paradise, yet it did not occur to him to question, as a white man would have done, whether the angel with the flaming sword had authority for her action. Neither did he lay the blame for things gone wrong upon any woman. He simply made up his mind to make the best of what was.

VII

It had been a peaceful week in the Wou household—the week before little Yen was to enter the American school. So peaceful indeed that Wou Sankwei had begun to think that his wife was reconciled to his wishes with regard to the boy. He whistled softly as he whittled away at a little ship he was making for him. Adah Charlton's suggestions had set coursing a train of thought which had curved around Pau Lin so closely that he had decided that, should she offer any further opposition to the boy's attending the American school, he would not insist upon it. After all, though the American language might be useful during this century, the wheel of the world would turn again, and then it might not be necessary at all. Who could tell? He came very near to expressing himself thus to Pau Lin.

And now it was the evening before the morning that little Yen was to march away to the American school. He had been excited all day over the prospect, and to calm him, his father finally told him to read aloud a little story from the Chinese book which he had given him on his first birthday in America and which he had taught him to read. Obediently the little fellow drew his stool to his mother's side and read in his childish singsong the story of an irreverent lad who came to great grief because he followed after the funeral of his grandfather and regaled himself on the crisply roasted chickens and loose-skinned oranges which were left on the grave for the feasting of the spirit.

Wou Sankwei laughed heartily over the story. It reminded him of some of his own boyish escapades. But Pau Lin stroked silently the head of the little reader, and seemed lost in reverie.

A whiff of fresh salt air blew in from the bay. The mother shivered, and Wou Sankwei, looking up from the fastening of the boat's rigging, bade Yen close the door. As the little fellow came back to his mother's side, he stumbled over her knee.

"Oh, poor mother!" he exclaimed with quaint apology. "'Twas the stupid feet, not Yen."

"So," she replied, curling her arm around his neck, "'tis always the feet. They are to the spirit as the cocoon to the butterfly. Listen, and I will sing you the song of the Happy Butterfly."

She began singing the old Chinese ditty in a fresh birdlike voice. Wou Sankwei, listening, was glad to hear her. He liked having everyone around him cheerful and happy. That had been the charm of the Dean household.

The ship was finished before the little family retired. Yen examined it, critically at first, then exultingly. Finally, he carried it away and placed it carefully in the closet where he kept his kites, balls, tops, and other treasures. "We will set sail with it tomorrow after school," said he to his father, hugging gratefully that father's arm.

Sankwei rubbed the little round head. The boy and he were great chums.

———

What was that sound which caused Sankwei to start from his sleep? It was just on the borderland of night and day, an unusual time for Pau Lin to be up. Yet, he could hear her voice in Yen's room. He raised himself on his elbow and listened. She was softly singing a nursery song about some little squirrels and a huntsman. Sankwei wondered at her singing in that way at such an hour. From where he lay he could just perceive the child's cot and the silent child figure lying motionless in the dim light. How very motionless! In a moment Sankwei was beside it.

The empty cup with its dark dregs told the tale.

The thing he loved the best in all the world—the darling son who had crept into his heart with his joyousness and beauty—had been taken from him, by her who had given.

Sankwei reeled against the wall. The kneeling figure by the cot arose. The face of her was solemn and tender.

"He is saved," smiled she, "from the Wisdom of the New."

In grief too bitter for words the father bowed his head upon his hands.

"Why? Why?" queried Pau Lin, gazing upon him bewilderedly. "The child is happy. The butterfly mourns not o'er the shed cocoon."

Sankwei put up his shutters and wrote this note to Adah Charlton:

> *I have lost my boy through an accident. I am returning to China with my wife whose health requires a change.*

"ITS WAVERING IMAGE"

I

Pan was a half-white, half-Chinese girl. Her mother was dead, and Pan lived with her father who kept an Oriental Bazaar on Dupont Street. All her life had Pan lived in Chinatown, and if she were different in any sense from those around her, she gave little thought to it. It was only after the coming of Mark Carson that the mystery of her nature began to trouble her.

They met at the time of the boycott of the Sam Yups by the See Yups. After the heat and dust and unsavoriness of the highways and byways of Chinatown, the young reporter who had been sent to find a story had stepped across the threshold of a cool, deep room, fragrant with the odor of dried lilies and sandalwood, and found Pan.

She did not speak to him, nor he to her. His business was with the spectacled merchant, who, with a pointed brush, was making up accounts in brown paper books and rolling balls in an abacus box. As to Pan, she always turned from whites. With her father's people she was natural and at home; but in the presence of her mother's she felt strange and constrained, shrinking from their curious scrutiny as she would from the sharp edge of a sword.

When Mark Carson returned to the office, he asked some questions concerning the girl who had puzzled him. What was she? Chinese or white? The city editor answered him, adding: "She is an unusually bright girl, and could tell more stories about the Chinese than any other person in this city—if she would."

Mark Carson had a determined chin, clever eyes, and a tone to his voice which easily won for him the confidence of the unwary. In the reporter's room he was spoken of as "a man who would sell his soul for a story."

After Pan's first shyness had worn off, he found her bewilderingly frank and free with him; but he had all the instincts of a gentleman save one, and made no ordinary mistake about her. He was Pan's first white friend. She was born a Bohemian, exempt from the conventional restrictions imposed upon either the white or Chinese woman; and the Oriental who was her father mingled with his affection for his child so great a respect for and trust in the daughter of the dead white woman, that everything she did or said was right to him. And Pan herself! A white woman might pass over an insult; a Chinese woman fail to see one. But Pan! He would be a brave man indeed who offered one to childish little Pan.

All this Mark Carson's clear eyes perceived, and with delicate tact and subtlety he taught the young girl that, all unconscious until his coming, she had lived her life alone. So well did she learn this lesson that it seemed at times as if her white self must entirely dominate and trample under foot her Chinese.

Meanwhile, in full trust and confidence, she led him about Chinatown, initiating him into the simple mystery and history of many things for which she, being of her father's race, had a tender regard and pride. For her sake he was received as a brother by the yellow-robed priest in the joss house, the Astrologer of Prospect Place, and other conservative Chinese. The Water Lily Club opened its doors to him when she knocked, and the Sublimely Pure Brothers organization admitted him as one of its honorary members, thereby enabling him not only to see but to take part in a ceremony in which no American had ever before participated. With her by his side, he was welcomed wherever he went. Even the little Chinese women in the midst of their babies received him with gentle smiles, and the children solemnly munched his candies and repeated nursery rhymes for his edification.

He enjoyed it all, and so did Pan. They were both young and

light-hearted. And when the afternoon was spent, there was always that high room open to the stars, with its China bowls full of flowers and its big colored lanterns, shedding a mellow light.

Sometimes there was music. A Chinese band played three evenings a week in the gilded restaurant beneath them, and the louder the gongs sounded and the fiddlers fiddled, the more delighted was Pan. Just below the restaurant was her father's bazaar. Occasionally Mun You would stroll upstairs and inquire of the young couple if there was anything needed to complete their felicity, and Pan would answer: "Thou only." Pan was very proud of her Chinese father. "I would rather have a Chinese for a father than a white man," she often told Mark Carson. The last time she had said that, he had asked whom she would prefer for a husband, a white man or a Chinese. And Pan, for the first time since he had known her, had no answer for him.

II

It was a cool, quiet evening, after a hot day. A new moon was in the sky.

"How beautiful above! How unbeautiful below!" exclaimed Mark Carson involuntarily.

He and Pan had been gazing down from their open retreat into the lantern-lighted, motley-thronged street beneath them.

"Perhaps it isn't very beautiful," replied Pan, "but it is here I live. It is my home." Her voice quivered a little.

He leaned toward her suddenly and grasped her hands.

"Pan," he cried, "you do not belong here. You are white—white."

"No! no!" protested Pan.

"You are," he asserted. "You have no right to be here."

"I was born here," she answered, "and the Chinese people look upon me as their own."

"But they do not understand you," he went on. "Your real self is alien to them. What interest have they in the books you read—the thoughts you think?"

"They have an interest in me," answered faithful Pan. "Oh, do not speak in that way anymore."

"But I must," the young man persisted. "Pan, don't you see that you have got to decide what you will be—Chinese or white? You cannot be both."

"Hush! Hush!" bade Pan. "I do not love you when you talk to me like that."

A little Chinese boy brought tea and saffron cakes. He was a picturesque little fellow with a quaint manner of speech. Mark Carson jested merrily with him, while Pan holding a tea-bowl between her two small hands laughed and sipped.

When they were alone again, the silver stream and the crescent moon became the objects of their study. It was a very beautiful evening.

After a while Mark Carson, his hand on Pan's shoulder, sang:

"And forever, and forever,
As long as the river flows,
As long as the heart has passions,
As long as life has woes,
The moon and its broken reflection,
And its shadows shall appear,
As the symbol of love in heaven,
And its wavering image here."

Listening to that irresistible voice singing her heart away, the girl broke down and wept. She was so young and so happy.

"Look up at me," bade Mark Carson. "Oh, Pan! Pan! Those tears prove that you are white."

Pan lifted her wet face.

"Kiss me, Pan," said he. It was the first time.

Next morning Mark Carson began work on the special-feature article which he had been promising his paper for some weeks.

III

"Cursed be his ancestors," bayed Man You.

He cast a paper at his daughter's feet and left the room.

Startled by her father's unwonted passion, Pan picked up the paper, and in the clear passionless light of the afternoon read that which forever after was blotted upon her memory.

"Betrayed! Betrayed! Betrayed to be a betrayer!"

It burnt red hot; agony unrelieved by words, unassuaged by tears.

So till evening fell. Then she stumbled up the dark stairs which led to the high room open to the stars and tried to think it out. Someone had hurt her. Who was it? She raised her eyes. There shone: "Its Wavering Image." It helped her to lucidity. He had done it. Was it unconsciously dealt—that cruel blow? Ah, well did he know that the sword which pierced her through others, would carry to her own heart the pain of all those others. None knew better than he that she, whom he had called "a white girl, a white woman," would rather that her own naked body and soul had been exposed, than that things, sacred and secret to those who loved her, should be cruelly unveiled and ruthlessly spread before the ridiculing and uncomprehending foreigner. And knowing all this so well, so well, he had carelessly sung her heart away, and with her kiss upon his lips, had smilingly turned and stabbed her. She, who was of the race that remembers.

IV

Mark Carson, back in the city after an absence of two months, thought of Pan. He would see her that very evening. Dear little Pan, pretty Pan, clever Pan, amusing Pan; Pan, who was always so frankly glad to have him come to her; so eager to hear all that he was doing; so appreciative, so inspiring, so loving. She would have forgotten that article by now. Why should a white woman care about such things? Her true self was above it all. Had he not taught her *that* during the weeks in which they had seen so much of one another? True, his last lesson had been a little harsh, and as yet he knew not how she had taken it; but even if its roughness had hurt and irritated, there was a healing balm, a wizard's oil which none knew so well as he how to apply.

But for all these soothing reflections, there was an undercurrent of feeling which caused his steps to falter on his way to Pan. He turned into Portsmouth Square and took a seat on one of the benches facing the fountain erected in memory of Robert Louis Stevenson. Why had Pan failed to answer the note he had written telling her of the assignment which would keep him out of town for a couple of months and giving her his address? Would Robert Louis Stevenson have known why? Yes—and so did Mark Carson. But though Robert Louis Stevenson would have boldly answered himself the question, Mark Carson thrust it aside, arose, and pressed up the hill.

"I knew they would not blame you, Pan!"

"Yes."

"And there was no word of you, dear. I was careful about that, not only for your sake, but for mine."

Silence.

"It is mere superstition anyway. These things have got to be exposed and done away with."

Still silence.

Mark Carson felt strangely chilled. Pan was not herself tonight. She did not even look herself. He had been accustomed to seeing her in American dress. Tonight she wore the Chinese costume. But for her clear-cut features she might have been a Chinese girl. He shivered.

"Pan," he asked, "why do you wear that dress?"

Within her sleeves Pan's small hands struggled together; but her face and voice were calm.

"Because I am a Chinese woman," she answered.

"You are not," cried Mark Carson, fiercely. "You cannot say that now, Pan. You are a white woman—white. Did your kiss not promise me that?"

"A white woman!" echoed Pan, her voice rising high and clear to the stars above them. "I would not be a white woman for all the world. *You* are a white man. And *what* is a promise to a white man!"

———

When she was lying low, the element of Fire having raged so fiercely within her that it had almost shriveled up the childish frame, there came to the house of Man You a little toddler who could scarcely speak. Climbing upon Pan's couch, she pressed her head upon the sick girl's bosom. The feel of that little head brought tears.

"Lo!" said the mother of the toddler. "Thou wilt bear a child thyself someday, and all the bitterness of this will pass away."

And Pan, being a Chinese woman, was comforted.

THE GIFT OF LITTLE ME

The schoolroom was decorated with banners and flags wrought in various colors. Chinese lanterns swung overhead. A big, green porcelain frog with yellow eyes squatted in the center of the teacher's desk. Tropical and native plants: azaleas, hyacinths, palms, and Chinese lilies, filled the air with their fragrance.

It was the day before the Chinese New Year of 18—and Miss McLeod's little scholars, in the decoration of their schoolroom, had expressed their love of quaint conceits and their appreciation of the beautiful. They were all in holiday attire. There was Han Wenti in sky-hued raiment and loose, flowing sleeves, upon each of which was embroidered a yellow dragon. Han Wenti's father was the Chief of his clan in America. There was San Kee, the son of the Americanized merchant, stiff and slim in American store clothes. Little Choy, on the girls' side, proudly wore a checked louisine Mother Hubbard gown, while Fei and Sie looked like hummingbirds in their native costume of bright-colored silks flowered with gold.

Miss McLeod's eyes wandered over the heap of gifts piled on three chairs before her desk, and over the heads of the young givers, to where on a back seat a little fellow in a blue cotton tunic and pantaloons sat swinging a pair of white-soled shoes in a "don't care for anybody" fashion.

Little Me was looked upon almost as a criminal by his schoolfellows. He was the only scholar in all the school who failed to offer at the shrine of the Teacher, and the fact that he was the son of a man who dined on no richer dish than rice and soy gravy did not palliate his offense. There were other scholars who knew not the taste of mushrooms, bamboo shoots, and suckling pigs, yet who were unceasing in their offerings of paper mats, wildflowers, pebbles, strange insects, and other gifts possessing at least a sentimental value. The truth of the matter, however, was that Little Me was neither unappreciative nor unloving. He was simply afflicted with pride. If he could not give in the princely fashion of Hom Hing and Lee Chu, the sons of the richest merchants in Chinatown, he would not give at all.

Yet if Miss McLeod, in her Scotch heart, allowed herself a favorite amongst her scholars, it was Little Me. Many a time had she incurred the displeasure of the parents of Hom Hing and Lee Chu by rejecting the oft-times valuable presents of their chubby, complacent-faced sons. She had seen Little Me's eyes cloud and his small hands draw up in his sleeves when the pattering footsteps of the braided darlings of the rich led them, with their offerings, to her desk.

"Attention, children!" said Miss McLeod; and she made a little speech in which she thanked her scholars for their tokens of appreciation and affection, but impressed upon them that she prized as much a wooden image of his own carving from a boy who had nothing more to offer, as she did an ivory or jade figure from one whose father could afford to wear gold buttons; that a lychee from the orphan Amoy was as refreshing to her as a basket of oranges from the only daughter of the owner of many fruit ranches. The greatest of all gifts was beyond price. They must remember the story she had told them at Christmastime of the giving of a darling and only Son to a loved people. All the money in the world could not have paid for that dear little boy. He was a free gift.

Little Me stopped swinging his feet in their white-soled shoes. With solemn eyes and puckered brow he meditated over this speech.

—

The first day of the new year was kept with much rejoicing. There were gay times under the lanterns, quaint ceremonies, and fine feasting. The flutist came out with his flute, the banjo man with his banjo, and the fiddler with his fiddle. No child but had a piece of gold or silver given to him or her, and sweetmeats, loose-skinned oranges, and watermelon seeds were scattered around galore. Strains of music enlivened the dark alleys, and "flowers" or fireworks delighted both old and young. The Literary and Benevolent Societies brought forth those of their number whose imaginations and experiences gave them the power to portray the achievements of heroes, the despair of lovers, the blessings which fall to the lot of the filial son, and the terrible fate of the undutiful, and while the sun went down and long after it had set, groups of fascinated youths sat listening to tales of magic and enchantment.

In the midst of it all Little Me wandered around in his white-soled shoes, and thought of that other story—the story of the Babe.

On the second day of the Chinese New Year, Miss McLeod, her twine bag full to overflowing with little red parcels of joy, stopped before the door of the Chee house. As there was no response to her knock, she lifted the latch and entered a darkened room. By a couch in the farthest corner of the room a woman knelt, moaning and tearful. It was Chee A Tae, Little Me's mother. Little Me's proper name was Chee Ping. Miss McLeod touched her shoulder sympathetically. The woman shuddered and the low moans became heart-rending cries and sobs. Did the teacher know that her baby was stolen? Some evil spirit had witched him away. Her husband, with some friends, was searching for the child; but she felt sure they would find him—never. She had burnt incense to "Mother" and besought the aid of the goddess of children; but her prayers would not avail, because her husband had neglected that month to send his parents cash for ginseng and broth. He had tried his luck with the Gambling Cash Tiger and failed. Had he been fortunate, his parents would have received twice their usual portion, but as it was, he had lost. And now the baby, the younger brother of Little Me, was lost too.

"How did it happen?" inquired Miss McLeod.

"We were alone—the babe and I," replied the mother. "My man was visiting and Little Me was playing in the alley. I stepped over with a bowl of boiled rice and a pot of tea for old Sien Tau. We have not much for our own mouths, but it is well to begin the New Year by being kind to those who may not see another. The babe was sleeping when I last beheld him. When I returned, whether he was asleep, awake, in the land of the living or in the spirit world, was withheld from me. A wolf—a tiger heart—alone knew."

This was truly a case needing sympathy. Miss McLeod did her best, and after a while Chee A Tae sat up and listened with some hope for her husband's footsteps. He came at last, a tired, gaunt-looking man, wearing in the face of the holiday, the blue cotton blouse and pantaloons of a working Chinaman, and a very dilapidated American slouch hat, around which he had wound his queue. He was followed into the room by several of his countrymen, who cast suspicious glances at the white woman present but upon recognition came forward, each in turn, and saluted her in American fashion. There were several points of difference between Miss McLeod and the other white teachers of Chinatown which had won for her the special favor of her pupils' parents. One was that though it was plain to all that she loved her work and taught the children committed to her charge with the utmost patience and care, she was not a child-cuddling and caressing woman. Another, that she had taken pains to learn the Chinese language before attempting to teach her own. Thirdly, she lived in Chinatown, and made herself at home amongst its denizens.

Chee A Tae was bitterly disappointed at seeing her husband without the babe. She arose from her couch, and pulling open the door, which the men had closed behind them, pointed them out again, crying: "Go, find my son! Go, find my son!"

Chee Ping the First turned upon her resentfully. "Woman," he cried, "that he is lost is your fault. I have searched with my eyes, ears, tongue, and limbs; but one might as well look for a pin at the bottom of the ocean."

The mother began to weep pitifully. "'Tis the Gambling Cash Tiger," she sobbed. "'Twas he who caused you to forget your parents, and ill fortune has followed therefor. A-ya, a-ya, a-ya. My heart is as heavy as the blackest heavens!"

"What nonsense!" exclaimed Miss McLeod, thinking it time to interfere. "The child cannot be far away. Let us all hunt and see who will find him first."

A crowd of men, women, and children had gathered outside the door, most of them in gay holiday attire. At these words of the teacher there was an assenting babel of voices, followed by a darting into passages, up stairways, and behind doors. Lanterns were lit for the exploration of underground cellars, stores, closets, stairways, balconies. Not a hole in the vicinity of the Chee dwelling but was penetrated by keen eyes. Rich and poor alike joined in the search, a yellow-robed priest from the joss house and one of the Chiefs of the Six Companies being conspicuously interested.

The mother, following in the footsteps of Miss McLeod, kept up a plaintive wailing. "A-ya, my young bud, my jade jewel, my peach bloom. Little hands, veined like young leaves; voice like the breath of a zephyr. Alas, the fates are against me! You are lost to your poor mother who is without resource and bound with fetters. Death would be sweet indeed; but that boon is denied."

The day wore on and evening gradually stole upon them, followed by night. The wind blew in gusts, but the moon had risen and was shining bright so that there was a kind of moonlight even in the dark alleys. The main portion of Chinatown had been thoroughly scoured, and most attention was now being given to the hills which crept up to Powell Street. It was in a top story of a halfway hill tenement that Miss McLeod's room was located; a cozy little place, for all its apparently comfortless environment. When the wind began to blow bleak from the bay, her thoughts drifted longingly to her easy chair and cheery grate fire; but only for a moment. Until the baby was found she could know no rest. The distress of these Chinese people was hers; their troubles also. Had she not adopted them as her own when kinfolk had failed her? Their grateful appreciation of the smallest service; their undemonstrative but faithful affection had been as balm to a heart wounded by the indifference and bruised by the ingratitude of those to whom she had devoted her youth, her strength, and her abilities.

Suddenly a cry was heard. Wang Hom Hing, a merchant Chinaman, who had taken command of the search party detailed to explore the upper part of Chinatown, appeared at the door of a rickety tenement—the one in which Miss McLeod had built her nest—and waved, under the lanterns, a Chinese flag, signal that the child was found.

Pell-mell the Chinese rushed toward their country's emblem. With the exception of Miss McLeod, not a single white person, not even a policeman, had been impressed into the search.

Leading the rushing crowd was Chee Ping the First; in the midst panted A Tae and her white woman friend, and in the wake of all calmly and quietly pattered Little Me. Though usually the chief object of his parents' attention, this day, or rather night, he seemed altogether forgotten.

Up several flights of stairs streamed the searchers, while from every door on the landings, men, women, and children peered out, inquiring what it all meant. Hemmed in by numbers, the teacher found herself at last blocked outside her own room.

Someone was talking loudly and excitedly. It was Wang Hom Hing, the father of her pupil of that name, and the uncle of another pupil, Lee Chu. What was he saying? The teacher strained her ears to catch his words. Gracious Heavens! He was declaring that she had stolen the child; that it lay in her room, hidden under the coverlets of her bed—positive evidence that she, who, under the guise of friendship, had ingratiated herself into their hearts and homes, was in reality a secret enemy.

"Trust her no more—this McLeod, Jean," he cried. "Though her smile is as sweet as honey, her heart is like a razor."

There was an ominous silence after this speech.

Wang Hom Hing was a pompous man whose conceit had been inflated by the flattery of wily white people, who, unlike the undiplomatic Scotch woman, did discriminate between the gifts of the rich and poor. Nevertheless, as President of the Water Lily Club and Secretary of the Society of Celestial Reason, he was a man of influence in Chinatown, and this was painfully impressed upon the teacher when Chee A Tae cast upon her a shuddering glance and fell swooning into the arms of a stout countrywoman behind her.

Now, the blood of Scottish chieftains throbbed in Miss McLeod's veins; and it was this brave blood which, when all the ships in which she had stored her early hopes and dreams had one by one been lost, had borne up her soul above the stormy flood, and helped her to launch another ship in a sea both wild and strange. That ship had weathered many a gale. Should she, after steering it safely into port, allow it to founder—in harbor? Never! That ship was the safe-deposit bank for all her womanly affection and energy. It carried her Chinese work—the work in which she had found consolation, peace, and happiness. Hom Hing should not wreck it without some effort on her part to save.

The intrepid woman, nerved by these thoughts, pushed through the human wall before her and reached the speaker's side. Sleeping in the midst of the tumult lay the babe, its little hand under its cheek. So pretty a picture that even in her stress and excitement she paused for a moment to wonder and admire.

Then she faced the big Chinaman in his gorgeous holiday robes, her small, slight form drawn to its fullest height, her light blue eyes ablaze.

"Wang Hom Hing," she cried. "You know you are trying to make my friends believe what you do not believe yourself! I know no more than its mother does about how the dear baby came here."

The Chinese merchant shrugged his shoulders insolently, and addressing the people again, asked them to judge for themselves. The child had been stolen. The teacher had pretended to aid in a search, yet it had been he and not she who had led the way to her room where it had been found.

Low mutterings were heard throughout the place; but after they had subsided, the white woman, looking around for a friendly face, was surprised and cheered to find many. Her spirits rose.

"How was I to know the child lay in my room?" she indignantly inquired. "I left the place in the early morning. It has been brought there since by someone unknown to me."

Wang Hom Hing laughed scornfully as he moved away, his revenge, as he thought, complete.

The father of the babe raised his son in his arms and passed him on to the mother, who stood with arms outstretched. Clutching the child convulsively, she gazed with horror-struck eyes at the teacher.

"Friends," cried the white woman raising her voice in a last effort, "will you allow that man to turn from me your hearts? Have you not known me long enough to believe that though I cannot explain to you how the baby came to be in my room, yet I am innocent of having brought it there. A Tae"—addressing the mother—"can you believe that I would harm one hair of your baby's head?"

A Tae hesitated, her eyes full of tears. She had loved the teacher, but Wang Hom Hing had sown a poisonous seed in her superstitious mind. Miss McLeod noted her hesitation with a sinking of the heart that was almost despair.

Up hobbled a very old and very tiny woman.

"McLeod, Jean," she cried, "your gracious and noble qualities of mind and soul merit a happier New Year's Day than this. Wang Hom Hing's words cannot deceive old Sien Tau."

Ah! The Scotch woman grasped gratefully the old Chinese woman's hand. She could not speak for the tickle in her throat.

Then spake A Tae: "Teacher, forgive me," besought she.

And the teacher smiled her answer.

A number of men and women came forward, looked into the teacher's face, thanked her for past kindnesses, and expressed their confidence in her.

"McLeod, Jean," declared an old man, "you are a hundred women good."

Which was the highest compliment that Jean McLeod had ever received.

"You are wrong, mother!" said she, turning with a beaming face to old Sien Tau. "This is the happiest day I have known."

Explained the father of the babe: "The gods, seeing my unworthiness, took from me to give to you."

And Little Me, straggling to the teacher's side, piped in the language she herself had taught him:

"I have one brother. I love him all over. You say baby boy best gift, so I give him to you when my father and mother not see. Little Me give better than Lee Chu and Hom Hing."

It was some time before the tumult occasioned by Little Me's boastful but sweet confession subsided. It had been heard by all, but was understood wholly by none save the teacher.

—

That when no watchful eye was there to see, the baby had been carried in Little Me's sturdy arms from under the home roof to the teacher's tenement room, was made plain to everyone by the child himself. But it devolved upon Miss McLeod, in order to save her little scholar from obviously justifiable paternal wrath, to explain his reason for the kidnapping, and this she did so clearly and eloquently that the father, raising his first born to his knee, declared in English: "I proud of him. He Number One scholar," while the mother fondly smiled.

Little Me looked at the baby in his mother's lap, and then at the teacher. His eyes filled with tears.

"You not like what I give you well enough to keep him," he sobbed.

"Yes, yes," consoled Miss McLeod. "I like him so well that I put him away in my heart where I keep the baby of my story. Don't you remember? That was what the Father of the story gave the baby for. To be kept in the people's hearts after he had gone back to Him!"

"Ah, yes," responded the child, his face brightening. "You keep my brother in your heart and I keep him in the house with me and my father and mother. That best of all!"

THE STORY OF ONE WHITE WOMAN WHO MARRIED A CHINESE

I

Why did I marry Liu Kanghi, a Chinese? Well, in the first place, because I loved him; in the second place, because I was weary of working, struggling and fighting with the world; in the third place, because my child needed a home.

My first husband was an American fifteen years older than myself. For a few months I was very happy with him. I had been a working girl—a stenographer. A home of my own filled my heart with joy. It was a pleasure to me to wait upon James, cook him nice little dinners and suppers, read to him little pieces from the papers and magazines, and sing and play to him my little songs and melodies. And for a few months he seemed to be perfectly contented. I suppose I was a novelty to him, he having lived a bachelor existence until he was thirty-four. But it was not long before he left off smiling at my little jokes, grew restive and cross when I teased him, and when I tried to get him to listen to a story in which I was interested and longed to communicate, he would bid me not bother him. I was quick to see the change and realize that there was a gulf of differences between us. Nevertheless, I loved and was proud of him. He was considered a very bright and well-informed man, and although his parents had been uneducated working people he had himself been through the public schools. He was also an omnivorous reader of socialistic and new-thought literature. Woman suffrage was one of his particular hobbies. Whenever I had a magazine around he would pick it up and read aloud to me the columns of advice to women who were ambitious to become comrades to men and walk shoulder to shoulder with their brothers. Once I ventured to remark that much as I admired a column of men keeping step together, yet men and women thus ranked would, to my mind, make a very unbeautiful and disorderly spectacle. He frowned and answered that I did not understand him, and was too frivolous. He would often draw my attention to newspaper reports concerning women of marked business ability and enterprise. Once I told him that I did not admire clever businesswomen, as I had usually found them, and so had other girls of my acquaintance, not nearly so kindhearted, generous, and helpful as the humble drudges of the world—the ordinary working women. His answer to this was that I was jealous and childish.

But, in spite of his unkind remarks and evident contempt for me, I wished to please him. He was my husband and I loved him. Many an afternoon, when through with my domestic duties, did I spend in trying to acquire a knowledge of labor politics, socialism, woman suffrage, and baseball, the things in which he was most interested.

It was hard work, but I persevered until one day. It was about six months after our marriage. My husband came home a little earlier than usual, and found me engaged in trying to work out problems in subtraction and addition. He laughed sneeringly. "Give it up, Minnie," said he. "You weren't built for anything but taking care of kids. Gee! But there's a woman at our place who has a head for figures that makes her worth over a hundred dollars a month. *Her* husband would have a chance to develop himself."

This speech wounded me. I knew it was James's ambition to write a book on social reform.

The next day, unknown to my husband, I called upon the wife of the man who had employed me as stenographer before I was married, and inquired of her whether she thought I could get back my old position.

"But, my dear," she exclaimed, "your husband is receiving a good salary! Why should you work?"

I told her that my husband had in mind the writing of a book on social reform, and I wished to help him in his ambition by earning some money toward its publication.

"Social reform!" she echoed. "What sort of social reformer is he who would allow his wife to work when he is well able to support her!"

She bade me go home and think no more of an office position. I was disappointed. I said: "Oh! I wish I could earn some money for James. If I were earning money, perhaps he would not think me so stupid."

"Stupid, my dear girl! You are one of the brightest little women I know," kindly comforted Mrs. Rogers.

But I knew differently and went on to tell her of my inability to figure with my husband how much he had made on certain sales, of my lack of interest in politics, labor questions, woman suffrage, and world reformation. "Oh!" I cried, "I am a narrow-minded woman. All I care for is for my husband to love me and be kind to me, for life to be pleasant and easy, and to be able to help a wee bit the poor and sick around me."

Mrs. Rogers looked very serious as she told me that there were differences of opinion as to what was meant by "narrow-mindedness," and that the majority of men had no wish to drag their wives into all their business perplexities, and found more comfort in a woman who was unlike rather than like themselves. Only that morning her husband had said to her: "I hate a woman who tries to get into every kink of a man's mind, and who must be forever at his elbow meddling with all his affairs."

I went home comforted. Perhaps after a while James would feel and see as did Mr. Rogers. Vain hope!

My child was six weeks old when I entered business life again as stenographer for Rutherford & Rutherford. My salary was fifty dollars a month—more than I had ever earned before, and James was well pleased, for he had feared that it would be difficult for me to obtain a paying place after having been out of practice for so long. This fifty dollars paid for all our living expenses, with the exception of rent, so that James would be able to put by his balance against the time when his book would be ready for publication.

He began writing his book, and Miss Moran the young woman bookkeeper at his place collaborated with him. They gave three evenings a week to the work, sometimes four. She came one evening when the baby was sick and James had gone for the doctor. She looked at the child with the curious eyes of one who neither loved nor understood children. "There is no necessity for its being sick," said she. "There must be an error somewhere." I made no answer, so she went on: "Sin, sorrow, and sickness all mean the same thing. We have no disease that we do not deserve, no trouble which we do not bring upon ourselves."

I did not argue with her. I knew that I could not; but as I looked at her standing there in the prime of her life and strength, broad-shouldered, masculine-featured, and, as it seemed to me, heartless, I disliked her more than I had ever disliked anyone before. My own father had died after suffering for many years from a terrible malady, contracted while doing his duty as a physician and surgeon. And my little innocent child! What had sin to do with its measles?

When James came in she discussed with him the baseball game which had been played that afternoon, and also a woman suffrage meeting which she had attended the evening before.

After she had gone he seemed to be quite exhilarated. "That's a great woman!" he remarked.

"I do not think so!" I answered him. "One who would take from the sorrowful and suffering their hope of a happier existence here-after, and add to their trials on earth by branding them as objects of aversion and contempt, is not only not a great woman but, to my mind, no woman at all."

He picked up a paper and walked into another room.

"What do you think now?" I cried after him.

"What would be the use of my explaining to you?" he returned. "You wouldn't understand."

How my heart yearned over my child those days! I would sit before the typewriter and in fancy hear her crying for her mother. Poor, sick little one, watched over by a strange woman, deprived of her proper nourishment. While I took dictation from my employer I thought only of her. The result, of course, was that I lost my place.

My husband showed his displeasure at this in various ways, and as the weeks went by and I was unsuccessful in obtaining another position, he became colder and more indifferent. He was neither a drinking nor an abusive man; but he could say such cruel and cutting things that I would a hundred times rather have been beaten and ill-used than compelled, as I was, to hear them. He even made me feel it a disgrace to be a woman and a mother. Once he said to me: "If you had had ambition of the right sort you would have perfected yourself in your stenography so that you could have taken cases in court. There's a little fortune in that business."

I was acquainted with a woman stenographer who reported divorce cases and who had described to me the work, so I answered: "I would rather die of hunger, my baby in my arms, than report divorce proceedings under the eyes of men in a courthouse."

"Other women, as good as you, have done and are doing it," he retorted.

"Other women, perhaps better than I, have done and are doing it," I replied, "but all women are not alike. I am not that kind."

"That's so," said he. "Well, they are the kind who are up to date. You are behind the times."

One evening I left James and Miss Moran engaged with their work and went across the street to see a sick friend. When I returned I let myself into the house very softly for fear of awakening the baby whom I had left sleeping. As I stood in the hall I heard my husband's voice in the sitting room. This is what he was saying:

"I am a lonely man. There is no companionship between me and my wife."

"Nonsense!" answered Miss Moran, as I thought a little impatiently. "Look over this paragraph, please, and tell me if you do not think it would be well to have it follow after the one ending with the words 'ultimate concord,' in place of that beginning with 'These great principles.'"

"I cannot settle my mind upon the work tonight," said James in a sort of thick, tired voice. "I want to talk to you—to win your sympathy—your love."

I heard a chair pushed back. I knew Miss Moran had arisen.

"Good night!" I heard her say. "Much as I would like to see this work accomplished, I shall come no more!"

"But, my God! You cannot throw the thing up at this late date."

"I can and I will. Let me pass, sir."

"If there were no millstone around my neck, you would not say, 'Let me pass, sir,' in that tone of voice."

The next I heard was a heavy fall. Miss Moran had knocked my big husband down.

I pushed open the door. Miss Moran, cool and collected, was pulling on her gloves. James was struggling to his feet.

"Oh, Mrs. Carson!" exclaimed the former. "Your husband fell over the stool. Wasn't it stupid of him!"

———

James, of course, got his divorce six months after I deserted him. He did not ask for the child, and I was allowed to keep it.

II

I was on my way to the waterfront, the baby in my arms. I was walking quickly, for my state of mind was such that I could have borne twice my burden and not have felt it. Just as I turned down a hill which led to the docks, someone touched my arm and I heard a voice say:

"Pardon me, lady; but you have dropped your baby's shoe!"

"Oh, yes!" I answered, taking the shoe mechanically from an outstretched hand, and pushing on.

I could hear the waves lapping against the pier when the voice again fell upon my ear.

"If you go any farther, lady, you will fall into the water!"

My answer was a step forward.

A strong hand was laid upon my arm and I was swung around against my will.

"Poor little baby," went on the voice, which was unusually soft for a man's. "Let me hold him!"

I surrendered my child to the voice.

"Better come over where it is light and you can see where to walk!"

I allowed myself to be led into the light.

Thus I met Liu Kanghi, the Chinese who afterward became my husband. I followed him, obeyed him, trusted him from the very first. It never occurred to me to ask myself what manner of man was succoring me. I only knew that he was a man, and that I was being cared for as no one had ever cared for me since my father died. And my grim determination to leave a world which had been cruel to me passed away—and in its place I experienced a strange calmness and content.

"I am going to take you to the house of a friend of mine," he said as he preceded me up the hill, the baby in his arms.

"You will not mind living with Chinese people?" he added.

An electric light under which we were passing flashed across his face.

I did not recoil—not even at first. It may have been because he was wearing American clothes, wore his hair cut, and, even to my American eyes, appeared a good-looking young man—and it may have been because of my troubles; but whatever it was I answered him, and I meant it: "I would much rather live with Chinese than Americans."

He did not ask me why, and I did not tell him until long afterward the story of my unhappy marriage, my desertion of the man who had made it impossible for me to remain under his roof; the shame of the divorce, the averted faces of those who had been my friends; the cruelty of the world; the awful struggle for an existence for myself and child; sickness followed by despair.

The Chinese family with which he placed me were kind, simple folk. The father had been living in America for more than twenty years. The family consisted of his wife, a grown daughter, and several small sons and daughters, all of whom had been born in America. They made me very welcome and adored the baby. Liu Jusong, the father, was a working jeweler; but, because of an accident by which he had lost the use of one hand, was partially incapacitated for work. Therefore, their family depended for maintenance chiefly upon their kinsman, Liu Kanghi, the Chinese who had brought me to them.

"We love much our cousin," said one of the little girls to me one day. "He teaches us so many games and brings us toys and sweets."

As soon as I recovered from the attack of nervous prostration which laid me low for over a month after being received into the Liu home, my mind began to form plans for my own and my child's maintenance. One morning I put on my hat and jacket and told Mrs. Liu I would go downtown and make an application for work as a stenographer at the different typewriting offices. She pleaded with me to wait a week longer—until, as she said, "your limbs are more fortified with strength"; but I assured her that I felt myself well able to begin to do for myself, and that I was anxious to repay some little part of the expense I had been to them.

"For all we have done for you," she answered, "our cousin has paid us doublefold."

"No money can recompense your kindness to myself and child," I replied; "but if it is your cousin to whom I am indebted for board and lodging, all the greater is my anxiety to repay what I owe."

When I returned to the house that evening, tired out with my quest for work, I found Liu Kanghi tossing ball with little Fong on the front porch.

Mrs. Liu bustled out to meet me and began scolding in motherly fashion.

"Oh, why you go downtown before you strong enough? See! You look all sick again!" said she.

She turned to Liu Kanghi and said something in Chinese. He threw the ball back to the boy and came toward me, his face grave and concerned.

"Please be so good as to take my cousin's advice," he urged.

"I am well enough to work now," I replied, "and I cannot sink deeper into your debt."

"You need not," said he. "I know a way by which you can quickly pay me off and earn a good living without wearing yourself out and leaving the baby all day. My cousin tells me that you can create most beautiful flowers on silk, velvet, and linen. Why not then you do some of that work for my store? I will buy all you can make."

"Oh!" I exclaimed, "I should be only too glad to do such work! But do you really think I can earn a living in that way?"

"You certainly can," was his reply. "I am requiring an embroiderer, and if you will do the work for me I will try to pay you what it is worth."

So I gladly gave up my quest for office work. I lived in the Liu Jusong house and worked for Liu Kanghi. The days, weeks, and months passed peacefully and happily. Artistic needlework had always been my favorite occupation, and when it became a source both of remuneration and pleasure, I began to feel that life was worth living, after all. I watched with complacency my child grow amongst the little Chinese children. My life's experience had taught me that the virtues do not all belong to the whites. I was interested in all that concerned the Liu household, became acquainted with all their friends, and lost altogether the prejudice against the foreigner in which I had been reared.

I had been living thus more than a year when, one afternoon as I was walking home from Liu Kanghi's store on Kearney Street, a parcel of silks and floss under my arm, and my little girl trudging by my side, I came face to face with James Carson.

"Well, now," said he, planting himself in front of me, "you are looking pretty well. How are you making out?"

I caught up my child and pushed past him without a word. When I reached the Liu house I was trembling in every limb, so great was my dislike and fear of the man who had been my husband.

About a week later a letter came to the house addressed to me. It read:

204 Buchanan Street

Dear Minnie,—If you are willing to forget the past and make up, I am, too. I was surprised to see you the other day, prettier than ever—and much more of a woman. Let me know your mind at an early date.

Your affectionate husband,
James

I ignored this letter, but a heavy fear oppressed me. Liu Kanghi, who called the evening of the day I received it, remarked as he arose to greet me that I was looking troubled, and hoped that it was not the embroidery flowers.

"It is the shadow from my big hat," I answered lightly. I was dressed for going downtown with Mrs. Liu, who was preparing her eldest daughter's trousseau.

"Someday," said Liu Kanghi earnestly, "I hope that you will tell to me all that is in your heart and mind."

I found comfort in his kind face.

"If you will wait until I return, I will tell you all tonight," I answered.

Strange as it may seem, although I had known Liu Kanghi now for more than a year, I had had little talk alone with him, and all he knew about me was what he had learned from Mrs. Liu; namely, that I was a divorced woman who, when saved from self-destruction, was homeless and starving.

That night, however, after hearing my story, he asked me to be his wife. He said: "I love you and would protect you from all trouble. Your child shall be as my own."

I replied: "I appreciate your love and kindness, but I cannot answer you just yet. Be my friend for a little while longer."

"Do you have for me the love feeling?" he asked.

"I do not know," I answered truthfully.

Another letter came. It was written in a different spirit from the first and contained a threat about the child.

There seemed but one course open to me. That was to leave my Chinese friends. I did. With much sorrow and regret I bade them goodbye, and took lodgings in a part of the city far removed from the outskirts of Chinatown where my home had been with the Lius. My little girl pined for her Chinese playmates, and I myself felt strange and lonely; but I knew that if I wished to keep my child I could no longer remain with my friends.

I still continued working for Liu Kanghi, and carried my embroidery to his store in the evening after the little one had been put to sleep. He usually escorted me back; but never asked to be allowed, and I never invited him, to visit me, or even enter the house. I was a young woman, and alone, and what I had suffered from scandal since I had left James Carson had made me wise.

It was a cold, wet evening in November when he accosted me once again. I had run over to a delicatessen store at the corner of the block where I lived. As I stepped out, his burly figure loomed up in the gloom before me. I started back with a little cry, but he grasped my arm and held it.

"Walk beside me quietly if you do not wish to attract attention," said he, "and by God, if you do, I will take the kid tonight!"

"You dare not!" I answered. "You have no right to her whatever. She is my child and I have supported her for the last two years alone."

"Alone! What will the judges say when I tell them about the Chinaman?"

"What will the judges say!" I echoed. "What can they say? Is there any disgrace in working for a Chinese merchant and receiving pay for my labor?"

"And walking in the evening with him, and living for over a year in a house for which he paid the rent. Ha ha ha! Ha ha ha!"

His laugh was low and sneering. He had evidently been making enquiries concerning the Liu family, and also watching me for some time. How a woman can loathe and hate the man she has once loved!

We were nearing my lodgings. Perhaps the child had awakened and was crying for me. I would not, however, have entered the house, had he not stopped at the door and pushed it open.

"Lead the way upstairs!" said he. "I want to see the kid."

"You shall not," I cried. In my desperation I wrenched myself from his grasp and faced him, blocking the stairs.

"If you use violence," I declared, "the lodgers will come to my assistance. They know me!"

He released my arm.

"Bah!" said he. "I've no use for the kid. It is you I'm after getting reconciled to. Don't you know, Minnie, that once your husband, always your husband? Since I saw you the other day on the street, I have been more in love with you than ever before. Suppose we forget all and begin over again!"

Though the tone of his voice had softened, my fear of him grew greater. I would have fled up the stairs had he not again laid his hand on my arm.

"Answer me, girl," said he.

And in spite of my fear, I shook off his hand and answered him: "No husband of mine are you, either legally or morally. And I have no feeling whatever for you other than contempt."

"Ah! So you have sunk!"—his expression was evil—"The oily little Chink has won you!"

I was no longer afraid of him.

"Won me!" I cried, unheeding who heard me. "Yes, honorably and like a man. And what are you that dare sneer at one like him. For all your six feet of grossness, your small soul cannot measure up to his great one. You were unwilling to protect and care for the woman who was your wife or the little child you caused to come into this world; but he succored and saved the stranger woman, treated her as a woman, with reverence and respect; gave her child a home, and made them both independent, not only of others but of himself. Now, hearing you insult him behind his back, I know, what I did not know before—that I love him, and all I have to say to you is, Go!"

And James Carson went. I heard of him again but once. That was when the papers reported his death of apoplexy while exercising at a public gymnasium.

Loving Liu Kanghi, I became his wife, and though it is true that there are many Americans who look down upon me for so becoming, I have never regretted it. No, not even when men cast upon me the glances they cast upon sporting women. I accept the lot of the American wife of a humble Chinaman in America. The happiness of the man who loves me is more to me than the approval or disapproval of those who in my dark days left me to die like a dog. My Chinese husband has his faults. He is hot-tempered and, at times, arbitrary; but he is always a man, and has never sought to take away from me the privilege of being but a woman. I can lean upon and trust in him. I feel him behind me, protecting and caring for me, and that, to an ordinary woman like myself, means more than anything else.

Only when the son of Liu Kanghi lays his little head upon my bosom do I question whether I have done wisely. For my boy, the son of the Chinese man, is possessed of a childish wisdom which brings the tears to my eyes; and as he stands between his father and myself, like yet unlike us both, so will he stand in after years between his father's and his mother's people. And if there is no kindliness nor understanding between them, what will my boy's fate be?

HER CHINESE HUSBAND

Sequel to the Story of the White Woman Who Married a Chinese

Now that Liu Kanghi is no longer with me, I feel that it will ease my heart to record some memories of him—if I can. The task, though calling to me, is not an easy one, so throng to my mind the invincible proofs of his love for me, the things he has said and done. My memories of him are so vivid and pertinacious, my thoughts of him so tender.

To my Chinese husband I could go with all my little troubles and perplexities; to him I could talk as women love to do at times of the past and the future, the mysteries of religion, of life and death. He was not above discussing such things with me. With him I was never strange or embarrassed. My Chinese husband was simple in his tastes. He liked to hear a good story, and though unlearned in a sense, could discriminate between the good and bad in literature. This came of his Chinese education. He told me one day that he thought the stories in the Bible were more like Chinese than American stories, and added: "If you had not told me what you have about it, I should say that it was composed by the Chinese." Music had a soothing though not a deep influence over him. It could not sway his mind, but he enjoyed it just as he did a beautiful picture. Because I was interested in fancy work, so also was he. I can see his face, looking so grave and concerned, because one day by accident I spilt some ink on a piece of embroidery I was working. If he came home in the evenings and found me tired and out of sorts, he would cook the dinner himself, and go about it in such a way that I felt that he rather enjoyed showing off his skill as a cook. The next evening, if he found everything ready, he would humorously declare himself much disappointed that I was so exceedingly well.

At such times a gray memory of James Carson would arise. How his cold anger and contempt, as exhibited on like occasions, had shriveled me up in the long ago. And then—I would fall to musing on the difference between the two men as lovers and husbands.

James Carson had been much more of an ardent lover than ever had been Liu Kanghi. Indeed it was his passion, real or feigned, which had carried me off my feet. When wooing he had constantly reproached me with being cold, unfeeling, a marble statue, and so forth; and I, poor, ignorant little girl, would wonder how it was I appeared so when I felt so differently. For I had given James Carson my first love. Upon him my life had been concentrated as it has never been concentrated upon any other. Yet—!

There was nothing feigned about my Chinese husband. Simple and sincere as he was before marriage, so was he afterward. As my union with James Carson had meant misery, bitterness, and narrowness, so my union with Liu Kanghi meant, on the whole, happiness, health, and development. Yet the former, according to American ideas, had been an educated broad-minded man; the other, just an ordinary Chinaman.

But the ordinary Chinaman that I would show to you was the sort of man that children, birds, animals, and some women love. Every morning he would go to the window and call to his pigeons, and they would flock around him, hearing and responding to his whistling and cooing. The rooms we lived in had been his rooms ever since he had come to America. They were above his store, and large and cool. The furniture had been brought from China, but there was nothing of tinsel about it. Dark wood, almost black, carved and antique, some of the pieces set with mother-of-pearl. On one side of the inner room stood a case of books and an ancestral tablet. I have seen Liu Kanghi touch the tablet with reverence, but the faith of his fathers was not strong enough to cause him to bow before it. The elegant simplicity of these rooms had surprised me much when I was first taken to them. I looked at him then, standing for a moment by the window, a solitary pigeon peeking in at him, perhaps wondering who had come to divert from her her friend's attention. So had he lived since he had come to this country— quietly and undisturbed—from twenty years of age to twenty-five. I felt myself an intruder. A feeling of pity for the boy—for such he seemed in his enthusiasm—arose in my breast. Why had I come to confuse his calm? Was it ordained, as he declared?

My little girl loved him better than she loved me. He took great pleasure in playing with her, curling her hair over his fingers, tying her sash, and all the simple tasks from which so many men turn aside.

Once the baby got hold of a set rat trap, and was holding it in such a way that the slightest move would have released the spring and plunged the cruel steel into her tender arms. Kanghi's eyes and mine beheld her thus at the same moment. I stood transfixed with horror. Kanghi quietly went up to the child and took from her the trap. Then he asked me to release his hand. I almost fainted when I saw it. "It was the only way," said he. We had to send for the doctor, and even as it was, he came very near having a case of blood poisoning.

I have heard people say that he was a keen businessman, this Liu Kanghi, and I imagine that he was. I did not, however, discuss his business with him. All I was interested in were the pretty things and the women who would come in and jest with him. He could jest too. Of course, the women did not know that I was his wife. Once a woman in rich clothes gave him her card and asked him to call upon her. After she had left he passed the card to me. I tore it up. He took those things as a matter of course, and was not affected by them. "They are a part of Chinatown life," he explained.

He was a member of the Reform Club, a Chinese social club, and the Chinese Board of Trade. He liked to discuss business affairs and Chinese and American politics with his countrymen, and occasionally enjoyed an evening away from me. But I never needed to worry over him.

He had his littlenesses as well as his bignesses, had Liu Kanghi. For instance, he thought he knew better about what was good for my health and other things, purely personal, than I did myself, and if my ideas opposed or did not tally with his, he would very vigorously denounce what he called "the foolishness of women." If he admired a certain dress, he would have me wear it on every occasion possible, and did not seem to be able to understand that it was not always suitable.

"Wear the dress with the silver lines," he said to me one day somewhat authoritatively. I was attired for going out, but not as he wished to see me. I answered that the dress with the silver lines was unsuitable for a long and dusty ride on an open car.

"Never mind," said he, "whether it is unsuitable or not. I wish you to wear it."

"All right," I said. "I will wear it, but I will stay at home."

I stayed at home, and so did he.

At another time, he reproved me for certain opinions I had expressed in the presence of some of his countrymen. "You should not talk like that," said he. "They will think you are a bad woman."

My blood rose at that, and I answered him in a way which grieves me to remember. For Kanghi had never meant to insult or hurt me. Imperious by nature, he often spoke before he thought—and he was so boyishly anxious for me to appear in the best light possible before his own people.

There were other things too: a sort of childish jealousy and suspicion which it was difficult to allay. But a woman can forgive much to a man, the sincerity and strength of whose love makes her own, though true, seem slight and mean.

Yes, life with Liu Kanghi was not without its trials and tribulations. There was the continual uncertainty about his own life here in America, the constant irritation caused by the assumption of the white men that a white woman does not love her Chinese husband, and their actions accordingly; also sneers and offensive remarks. There was also on Liu Kanghi's side an acute consciousness that, though belonging to him as his wife, yet in a sense I was not his, but of the dominant race, which claimed me. This consciousness betrayed itself in words and ways which filled me with a passion of pain and humiliation. "Kanghi," I would sharply say, for I had to cloak my tenderness, "do not talk to me like that. You *are* my superior. . . . I would not love you if you were not."

But in spite of all I could do or say, it was there between us: that strange, invisible—what? Was it the barrier of race—that consciousness?

Sometimes he would talk about returning to China. The thought filled me with horror. I had heard rumors of secondary wives. One afternoon the cousin of Liu Kanghi, with whom I had lived, came to see me, and showed me a letter which she had received from a little Chinese girl who had been born and brought up in America until the age of ten. The last paragraph in the letter read: "Emma and I are very sad and wish we were back in America." Kanghi's cousin explained that the father of the little girls, having no sons, had taken to himself another wife, and the new wife lived with the little girls and their mother.

That was before my little boy was born. That evening I told Kanghi that he need never expect me to go to China with him.

"You see," I began, "I look upon you as belonging to me."

He would not let me say more. After a while he said: "It is true that in China a man may and occasionally does take a secondary wife, but that custom is custom, not only because sons are denied to the first wife, but because the first wife is selected by parents and guardians before a man is hardly a man. If a Chinese marries for love, his life is a filled-up cup, and he wants no secondary wife. No, not even for sake of a son. Take, for example, me, your great husband."

I sometimes commented upon his boyish ways and appearance, which was the reason why, when he was in high spirits, he would call himself my "great husband." He was not boyish always. I have seen him, when shouldering the troubles of kinfolk, the quarrels of his clan, and other responsibilities, acting and looking like a man of twice his years.

But for all the strange marriage customs of my husband's people I considered them far more moral in their lives than the majority of Americans. I expressed myself thus to Liu Kanghi, and he replied: "The American people think higher. If only more of them lived up to what they thought, the Chinese would not be so confused in try-ing to follow their leadership."

If ever a man rejoiced over the birth of his child, it was Liu Kanghi. The boy was born with a veil over his face. "A prophet!" cried the old mulatto Jewess who nursed me. "A prophet has come into the world."

She told this to his father when he came to look upon him, and he replied: "He is my son; that is all I care about." But he was so glad, and there was feasting and rejoicing with his Chinese friends for over two weeks. He came in one evening and found me weeping over my poor little boy. I shall never forget the expression on his face.

"Oh, shame!" he murmured, drawing my head down to his shoul-der. "What is there to weep about? The child is beautiful! The feel-ing heart, the understanding mind is his. And we will bring him up to be proud that he is of Chinese blood; he will fear none and, after him, the name of half-breed will no longer be one of contempt."

Kanghi as a youth had attended a school in Hong Kong, and while there had made the acquaintance of several half-Chinese, half-English lads. "They were the brightest of all," he told me, "but they lowered themselves in the eyes of the Chinese by being ashamed of their Chinese blood and ignoring it."

His theory, therefore, was that if his own son was brought up to be proud instead of ashamed of his Chinese half, the boy would become a great man.

Perhaps he was right, but he could not see as could I, an Ameri-can woman, the conflict before our boy.

After the little Kanghi had passed his first month, and we had found a reliable woman to look after him, his father began to take me around with him much more than formerly, and life became very enjoyable. We dined often at a Chinese restaurant kept by a friend of his, and afterward attended theaters, concerts, and other places of entertainment. We frequently met Americans with whom he had become acquainted through business, and he would intro-duce them with great pride in me shining in his eyes. The little jealousies and suspicions of the first year seemed no longer to irritate him, and though I had still cause to shrink from the gaze of strangers, I know that my Chinese husband was for several years a very happy man.

———

Now, I have come to the end. He left home one morning, followed to the gate by the little girl and boy (we had moved to a cottage in the suburbs).

"Bring me a red ball," pleaded the little girl.

"And me too," cried the boy.

"All right, chickens," he responded, waving his hand to them.

He was brought home at night, shot through the head. There are some Chinese, just as there are some Americans, who are opposed to all progress, and who hate with a bitter hatred all who would enlighten or be enlightened.

But that I have not the heart to dwell upon. I can only remember that when they brought my Chinese husband home there were two red balls in his pocket. Such was Liu Kanghi—a man.

THE AMERICANIZING OF PAU TSU

I

When Wan Hom Hing came to Seattle to start a branch of the merchant business which his firm carried on so successfully in the different ports of China, he brought with him his nephew, Wan Lin Fo, then eighteen years of age. Wan Lin Fo was a well-educated Chinese youth, with bright eyes and keen ears. In a few years' time he knew as much about the business as did any of the senior partners. Moreover, he learned to speak and write the American language with such fluency that he was never at a loss for an answer, when the white man, as was sometimes the case, sought to pose him. "All work and no play," however, is as much against the principles of a Chinese youth as it is against those of a young American, and now and again Lin Fo would while away an evening at the Chinese Literary Club, above the Chinese restaurant, discussing with some chosen companions the works and merits of Chinese sages—and some other things. New Year's Day, or rather, Week, would also see him, business forgotten, arrayed in national costume of finest silk, and color "the blue of the sky after rain," visiting with his friends, both Chinese and American, and scattering silver and gold coin amongst the youngsters of the families visited.

It was on the occasion of one of these New Year's visits that Wan Lin Fo first made known to the family of his firm's silent American partner, Thomas Raymond, that he was betrothed. It came about in this wise: One of the young ladies of the house, who was fair and frank of face and friendly and cheery in manner, observing as she handed him a cup of tea that Lin Fo's eyes wore a rather wistful expression, questioned him as to the wherefore:

"Miss Adah," replied Lin Fo, "may I tell you something?"

"Certainly, Mr. Wan," replied the girl. "You know how I enjoy hearing your tales."

"But this is no tale. Miss Adah, you have inspired in me a love—" Adah Raymond started. Wan Lin Fo spake slowly.

"For the little girl in China to whom I am betrothed."

"Oh, Mr. Wan! That is good news. But what have I to do with it?"

"This, Miss Adah! Every time I come to this house, I see you, so good and so beautiful, dispensing tea and happiness to all around, and I think, could I have in my home and ever by my side one who is also both good and beautiful, what a felicitous life mine would be!"

"You must not flatter me, Mr. Wan!"

"All that I say is founded on my heart. But I will speak not of you. I will speak of Pau Tsu."

"Pau Tsu?"

"Yes. That is the name of my future wife. It means a pearl."

"How pretty! Tell me all about her!"

"I was betrothed to Pau Tsu before leaving China. My parents adopted her to be my wife. As I remember, she had shining eyes and the good-luck color was on her cheek. Her mouth was like a red vine leaf, and her eyebrows most exquisitely arched. As slender as a willow was her form, and when she spoke, her voice lilted from note to note in the sweetest melody."

Adah Raymond softly clapped her hands.

"Ah! You were even then in love with her."

"No," replied Lin Fo thoughtfully. "I was too young to be in love—sixteen years of age. Pau Tsu was thirteen. But, as I have confessed, you have caused me to remember and love her."

Adah Raymond was not a self-conscious girl, but for the life of her she could think of no reply to Lin Wo's speech.

"I am twenty-two years old now," he continued. "Pau Tsu is eighteen. Tomorrow I will write to my parents and persuade them to send her to me at the time of the spring festival. My elder brother was married last year, and his wife is now under my parents' roof, so that Pau Tsu, who has been the daughter of the house for so many years, can now be spared to me."

"What a sweet little thing she must be," commented Adah Raymond.

"You will say that when you see her," proudly responded Lin Fo. "My parents say she is always happy. There is not a bird or flower or dewdrop in which she does not find some glad meaning."

"I shall be so glad to know her. Can she speak English?"

Lin Fo's face fell.

"No," he replied, "but,"—brightening—"when she comes I will have her learn to speak like you—and be like you."

II

Pau Tsu came with the spring, and Wan Lin Fo was one of the happiest and proudest of bridegrooms. The tiny bride was really very pretty—even to American eyes. In her peach and plum colored robes, her little arms and hands sparkling with jewels, and her shiny black head decorated with wonderful combs and pins, she appeared a bit of Eastern coloring amidst the Western lights and shades.

Lin Fo had not been forgotten, and her eyes under their downcast lids discovered him at once, as he stood awaiting her amongst a group of young Chinese merchants on the deck of the vessel.

The apartments he had prepared for her were furnished in American style, and her birdlike little figure in Oriental dress seemed rather out of place at first. It was not long, however, before she brought forth from the great box, which she had brought overseas, screens and fans, vases, panels, Chinese matting, artificial flowers and birds, and a number of exquisite carvings and pieces of antique porcelain. With these she transformed the American flat into an Oriental bower, even setting up in her sleeping-room a little chapel, enshrined in which was an image of the Goddess of Mercy, two ancestral tablets, and other emblems of her faith in the Gods of her fathers.

The Misses Raymond called upon her soon after arrival, and she smiled and looked pleased. She shyly presented each girl with a Chinese cup and saucer, also a couple of antique vases, covered with whimsical pictures, which Lin Fo tried his best to explain.

The girls were delighted with the gifts, and having fallen, as they expressed themselves, in love with the little bride, invited her through her husband to attend a launch party, which they intended giving the following Wednesday on Lake Washington.

Lin Fo accepted the invitation on behalf of himself and wife. He was quite at home with the Americans and, being a young man, enjoyed their rather effusive appreciation of him as an educated Chinaman. Moreover, he was of the opinion that the society of the American young ladies would benefit Pau Tsu in helping her to acquire the ways and language of the land in which he hoped to make a fortune.

Wan Lin Fo was a true son of the Middle Kingdom and secretly pitied all those who were born far away from its influences; but there was much about the Americans that he admired. He also entertained sentiments of respect for a motto which hung in his room which bore the legend: "When in Rome, do as the Romans do."

"What is best for men is also best for women in this country," he told Pau Tsu when she wept over his suggestion that she should take some lessons in English from a white woman.

"It may be best for a man who goes out in the street," she sobbed, "to learn the new language, but of what importance is it to a woman who lives only within the house and her husband's heart?"

It was seldom, however, that she protested against the wishes of Lin Fo. As her mother-in-law had said, she was a docile, happy little creature. Moreover, she loved her husband.

But as the days and weeks went by the girl bride whose life hitherto had been spent in the quiet retirement of a Chinese home in the performance of filial duties, in embroidery work and lute playing, in sipping tea and chatting with gentle girl companions, felt very much bewildered by the novelty and stir of the new world into which she had been suddenly thrown. She could not understand, for all Lin Fo's explanations, why it was required of her to learn the strangers' language and adopt their ways. Her husband's tongue was the same as her own. So also her little maid's. It puzzled her to be always seeing this and hearing that—sights and sounds which as yet had no meaning for her. Why also was it necessary to receive visitors nearly every evening?—visitors who could neither understand nor make themselves understood by her, for all their curious smiles and stares, which she bore like a second Vashti—or rather, Esther. And why, oh! why should she be constrained to eat her food with clumsy, murderous-looking American implements instead of with her own elegant and easily manipulated ivory chopsticks?

Adah Raymond, who at Lin Fo's request was a frequent visitor to the house, could not fail to observe that Pau Tsu's small face grew daily smaller and thinner, and that the smile with which she invariably greeted her, though sweet, was tinged with melancholy. Her woman's instinct told her that something was wrong, but what it was the light within her failed to discover. She would reach over to Pau Tsu and take within her own firm, white hand the small, trembling fingers, pressing them lovingly and sympathetically; and the little Chinese woman would look up into the beautiful face bent above hers and think to herself: "No wonder he wishes me to be like her!"

If Lin Fo happened to come in before Adah Raymond left he would engage the visitor in bright and animated conversation. They had so much of common interest to discuss, as is always the way with young people who have lived any length of time in a growing city of the West. But to Pau Tsu, pouring tea and dispensing sweetmeats, it was all Greek, or rather, all American.

"Look, my pearl, what I have brought you," said Lin Fo one afternoon as he entered his wife's apartments, followed by a messenger-boy, who deposited in the middle of the room a large cardboard box.

With murmurs of wonder Pau Tsu drew near, and the messenger-boy having withdrawn Lin Fo cut the string, and drew forth a beautiful lace evening dress and dark blue walking costume, both made in American style.

For a moment there was silence in the room. Lin Fo looked at his wife in surprise. Her face was pale and her little body was trembling, while her hands were drawn up into her sleeves.

"Why, Pau Tsu!" he exclaimed, "I thought to make you glad."

At these words the girl bent over the dress of filmy lace, and gathering the flounce in her hand smoothed it over her knee; then lifting a smiling face to her husband, replied: "Oh, you are too good, too kind to your unworthy Pau Tsu. My speech is slow, because I am overcome with happiness."

Then with exclamations of delight and admiration she lifted the dresses out of the box and laid them carefully over the couch.

"I wish you to dress like an American woman when we go out or receive," said her husband. "It is the proper thing in America to do as the Americans do. You will notice, light of my eyes, that it is only on New Year and our national holidays that I wear the costume of our country and attach a queue. The wife should follow the husband in all things."

A ripple of laughter escaped Pau Tsu's lips.

"When I wear that dress," said she, touching the walking costume, "I will look like your friend Miss Raymond."

She struck her hands together gleefully, but when her husband had gone to his business she bowed upon the floor and wept pitifully.

III

During the rainy season Pau Tsu was attacked with a very bad cough. A daughter of southern China, the chill, moist climate of the Puget Sound winter was very hard on her delicate lungs. Lin Fo worried much over the state of her health, and meeting Adah Raymond on the street one afternoon told her of his anxiety. The kindhearted girl immediately returned with him to the house. Pau Tsu was lying on her couch, feverish and breathing hard. The American girl felt her hands and head.

"She must have a doctor," said she, mentioning the name of her family's physician.

Pau Tsu shuddered. She understood a little English by this time.

"No! No! Not a man, *not* a man!" she cried.

Adah Raymond looked up at Lin Fo.

"I understand," said she. "There are several women doctors in this town. Let us send for one."

But Lin Fo's face was set.

"No!" he declared. "We are in America. Pau Tsu shall be attended to by your physician."

Adah Raymond was about to protest against this dictum when the sick wife, who had also heard it, touched her hand and whispered: "I not mind now. Man all right."

So the other girl closed her lips, feeling that if the wife would not dispute her husband's will it was not her place to do so; but her heart ached with compassion as she bared Pau Tsu's chest for the stethoscope.

"It was like preparing a lamb for slaughter," she told her sister afterward. "Pau Tsu was motionless, her eyes closed and her lips sealed, while the doctor remained; but after he had left and we two were alone she shuddered and moaned like one bereft of reason. I honestly believe that the examination was worse than death to that little Chinese woman. The modesty of generations of maternal ancestors was crucified as I rolled down the neck of her silk tunic."

It was a week after the doctor's visit, and Pau Tsu, whose cough had yielded to treatment, though she was still far from well, was playing on her lute, and whisperingly singing this little song, said to have been written on a fan which was presented to an ancient Chinese emperor by one of his wives:

"Of fresh new silk,
All snowy white,
And round as a harvest moon,
A pledge of purity and love,
A small but welcome boon.

While summer lasts,
When borne in hand,
Or folded on thy breast,
'Twill gently soothe thy burning brow,
And charm thee to thy rest.

But, oh, when Autumn winds blow chill,
And days are bleak and cold,
No longer sought, no longer loved,
'Twill lie in dust and mold.

This silken fan then deign accept,
Sad emblem of my lot,
Caressed and cherished for an hour,
Then speedily forgot."

"Why so melancholy, my pearl?" asked Lin Fo, entering from the street.

"When a bird is about to die, its notes are sad," returned Pau Tsu.

"But thou art not for death—thou art for life," declared Lin Fo, drawing her toward him and gazing into a face which day by day seemed to grow finer and more transparent.

IV

A Chinese messenger-boy ran up the street, entered the store of Wan Hom Hing & Co. and asked for the junior partner. When Lin Fo came forward he handed him a dainty, flowered missive, neatly folded and addressed. The receiver opened it and read:

Dear and Honored Husband,—Your Unworthy Pau Tsu lacks the
courage to face the ordeal before her. She has, therefore, left you and
prays you to obtain a divorce, as is the custom in America, so that you

may be happy with the Beautiful One, who is so much your Pau Tsu's superior. This, she acknowledges, for she sees with your eyes, in which, like a star, the Beautiful One shineth. Else, why should you have your Pau Tsu follow in her footsteps? She has tried to obey your will and to be as an American woman; but now she is very weary, and the terror of what is before her has overcome.

Your stupid thorn,
Pau Tsu

Mechanically Lin Fo folded the letter and thrust it within his breast pocket. A customer inquired of him the price of a lacquered tray. "I wish you good morning," he replied, reaching for his hat. The customer and clerks gaped after him as he left the store.

Out in the street, as fate would have it, he met Adah Raymond. He would have turned aside had she not spoken to him.

"Whatever is the matter with you, Mr. Wan?" she inquired. "You don't look yourself at all."

"The density of my difficulties you cannot understand," he replied, striding past her.

But Adah Raymond was persistent. She had worried lately over Pau Tsu.

"Something is wrong with your wife," she declared.

Lin Fo wheeled around.

"Do you know where she is?" he asked with quick suspicion.

"Why, no!" exclaimed the girl in surprise.

"Well, she has left me."

Adah Raymond stood incredulous for a moment, then with indignant eyes she turned upon the deserted husband.

"You deserve it!" she cried. "I have seen it for some time: your cruel, arbitrary treatment of the dearest, sweetest little soul in the world."

"I beg your pardon, Miss Adah," returned Lin Fo, "but I do not understand. Pau Tsu is heart of my heart. How then could I be cruel to her?"

"Oh, you stupid!" exclaimed the girl. "You're a Chinaman, but you're almost as stupid as an American. Your cruelty consisted in forcing Pau Tsu to be—what nature never intended her to be—an American woman; to adapt and adopt in a few months' time all our ways and customs. I saw it long ago, but as Pau Tsu was too sweet and meek to see any faults in her man I had not the heart to open her eyes—or yours. Is it not true that she has left you for this reason?"

"Yes," murmured Lin Fo. He was completely crushed. "And some other things."

"What other things?"

"She—is—afraid—of—the—doctor."

"She is!"—fiercely—"Shame upon you!"

Lin Fo began to walk on, but the girl kept by his side and continued:

"You wanted your wife to be an American woman while you remained a Chinaman. For all your clever adaptation of our American ways you are a thorough Chinaman. Do you think an American would dare treat his wife as you have treated yours?"

Wan Lin Fo made no response. He was wondering how he could ever have wished his gentle Pau Tsu to be like this angry woman. Now his Pau Tsu was gone. His anguish for the moment made him oblivious to the presence of his companion and the words she was saying. His silence softened the American girl. After all, men, even Chinamen, were nothing but big, clumsy boys, and she didn't believe in kicking a man after he was down.

"But, cheer up, you're sure to find her," said she, suddenly changing her tone. "Probably her maid has friends in Chinatown who have taken them in."

"If I find her," said Lin Fo fervently, "I will not care if she never speaks an American word, and I will take her for a trip to China, so that our son may be born in the country that Heaven loves."

"You cannot make too much amends for all she has suffered. As to Americanizing Pau Tsu—that will come in time. I am quite sure that were I transferred to your country and commanded to turn myself into a Chinese woman in the space of two or three months I would prove a sorry disappointment to whomever built their hopes upon me."

Many hours elapsed before any trace could be found of the missing one. All the known friends and acquaintances of little Pau Tsu were called upon and questioned; but if they had knowledge of the young wife's hiding place they refused to divulge it. Though Lin Fo's face was grave with an unexpressed fear, their sympathies were certainly not with him.

The seekers were about to give up the search in despair when a little boy, dangling in his hands a string of blue beads, arrested the attention of the young husband. He knew the necklace to be a gift from Pau Tsu to the maid, A-Toy. He had bought it himself. Stopping and questioning the little fellow he learned to his great joy that his wife and her maid were at the boy's home, under the care of his grandmother, who was a woman learned in herb lore.

Adah Raymond smiled in sympathy with her companion's evident great relief.

"Everything will now be all right," said she, following Lin Fo as he proceeded to the house pointed out by the lad. Arrived there, she suggested that the husband enter first and alone. She would wait a few moments.

"Miss Adah," said Lin Fo, "ten thousand times I beg your pardon, but perhaps you will come to see my wife some other time—not today?"

He hesitated, embarrassed and humiliated.

In one silent moment Adah Raymond grasped the meaning of all the morning's trouble—of all Pau Tsu's sadness.

"Lord, what fools we mortals be!" she soliloquized as she walked home alone. "I ought to have known. What else could Pau Tsu have thought?—coming from a land where women have no men friends save their husbands. How she must have suffered under her smiles! Poor, brave little soul!"

IN THE LAND OF THE FREE

I

"See, Little One—the hills in the morning sun. There is thy home for years to come. It is very beautiful and thou wilt be very happy there."

The Little One looked up into his mother's face in perfect faith. He was engaged in the pleasant occupation of sucking a sweetmeat; but that did not prevent him from gurgling responsively.

"Yes, my olive bud; there is where thy father is making a fortune for thee. Thy father! Oh, wilt thou not be glad to behold his dear face. 'Twas for thee I left him."

The Little One ducked his chin sympathetically against his mother's knee. She lifted him onto her lap. He was two years old, a round, dimple-cheeked boy with bright brown eyes and a sturdy little frame.

"Ah! Ah! Ah! Ooh! Ooh! Ooh!" puffed he, mocking a tugboat steaming by.

San Francisco's waterfront was lined with ships and steamers, while other craft, large and small, including a couple of white transports from the Philippines, lay at anchor here and there offshore. It was some time before the *Eastern Queen* could get docked, and even after that was accomplished, a lone Chinaman who had been waiting on the wharf for an hour was detained that much longer by men with the initials U.S.C. on their caps, before he could board the steamer and welcome his wife and child.

"This is thy son," announced the happy Lae Choo.

Hom Hing lifted the child, felt of his little body and limbs, gazed into his face with proud and joyous eyes; then turned inquiringly to a customs officer at his elbow.

"That's a fine boy you have there," said the man. "Where was he born?"

"In China," answered Hom Hing, swinging the Little One on his right shoulder, preparatory to leading his wife off the steamer.

"Ever been to America before?"

"No, not he," answered the father with a happy laugh.

The customs officer beckoned to another.

"This little fellow," said he, "is visiting America for the first time."

The other customs officer stroked his chin reflectively.

"Good day," said Hom Hing.

"Wait!" commanded one of the officers. "You cannot go just yet."

"What more now?" asked Hom Hing.

"I'm afraid," said the first customs officer, "that we cannot allow the boy to go ashore. There is nothing in the papers that you have shown us—your wife's papers and your own—having any bearing upon the child."

"There was no child when the papers were made out," returned Hom Hing. He spoke calmly; but there was apprehension in his eyes and in his tightening grip on his son.

"What is it? What is it?" quavered Lae Choo, who understood a little English.

The second customs officer regarded her pityingly.

"I don't like this part of the business," he muttered.

The first officer turned to Hom Hing and in an official tone of voice, said:

"Seeing that the boy has no certificate entitling him to admission to this country you will have to leave him with us."

"Leave my boy!" exclaimed Hom Hing.

"Yes; he will be well taken care of, and just as soon as we can hear from Washington he will be handed over to you."

"But," protested Hom Hing, "he is my son."

"We have no proof," answered the man with a shrug of his shoulders; "and even if so we cannot let him pass without orders from the Government."

"He is my son," reiterated Hom Hing, slowly and solemnly. "I am a Chinese merchant and have been in business in San Francisco for many years. When my wife told to me one morning that she dreamed of a green tree with spreading branches and one beautiful red flower growing thereon, I answered her that I wished my son to be born in our country, and for her to prepare to go to China. My wife complied with my wish. After my son was born my mother fell sick and my wife nursed and cared for her; then my father, too, fell sick, and my wife also nursed and cared for him. For twenty moons my wife care for and nurse the old people, and when they die they bless her and my son, and I send for her to return to me. I had no fear of trouble. I was a Chinese merchant and my son was my son."

"Very good, Hom Hing," replied the first officer. "Nevertheless, we take your son."

"No, you not take him; he my son too."

It was Lae Choo. Snatching the child from his father's arms she held and covered him with her own.

The officers conferred together for a few moments; then one drew Hom Hing aside and spoke in his ear.

Resignedly Hom Hing bowed his head, then approached his wife. "'Tis the law," said he, speaking in Chinese, "and 'twill be but for a little while—until tomorrow's sun arises."

"You, too," reproached Lae Choo in a voice eloquent with pain. But accustomed to obedience she yielded the boy to her husband, who in turn delivered him to the first officer. The Little One protested lustily against the transfer; but his mother covered her face with her sleeve and his father silently led her away. Thus was the law of the land complied with.

II

Day was breaking. Lae Choo, who had been awake all night, dressed herself, then awoke her husband. "'Tis the morn," she cried. "Go, bring our son."

The man rubbed his eyes and arose upon his elbow so that he could see out of the window. A pale star was visible in the sky. The petals of a lily in a bowl on the windowsill were unfurled.

"'Tis not yet time," said he, laying his head down again.

"Not yet time. Ah, all the time that I lived before yesterday is not so much as the time that has been since my little one was taken from me."

The mother threw herself down beside the bed and covered her face.

Hom Hing turned on the light, and touching his wife's bowed head with a sympathetic hand inquired if she had slept.

"Slept!" she echoed, weepingly. "Ah, how could I close my eyes with my arms empty of the little body that has filled them every night for more than twenty moons! You do not know—man—what it is to miss the feel of the little fingers and the little toes and the soft round limbs of your little one. Even in the darkness his darling eyes used to shine up to mine, and often have I fallen into slumber with his pretty babble at my ear. And now, I see him not; I touch him not; I hear him not. My baby, my little fat one!"

"Now! Now! Now!" consoled Hom Hing, patting his wife's shoulder reassuringly; "there is no need to grieve so; he will soon gladden you again. There cannot be any law that would keep a child from its mother!"

Lae Choo dried her tears.

"You are right, my husband," she meekly murmured. She arose and stepped about the apartment, setting things to rights. The box of presents she had brought for her California friends had been opened the evening before; and silks, embroideries, carved ivories, ornamental laquerware, brasses, camphorwood boxes, fans, and chinaware were scattered around in confused heaps. In the midst of unpacking the thought of her child in the hands of strangers had overpowered her, and she had left everything to crawl into bed and weep.

Having arranged her gifts in order she stepped out onto the deep balcony.

The star had faded from view and there were bright streaks in the western sky. Lae Choo looked down the street and around. Beneath the flat occupied by her and her husband were quarters for a number of bachelor Chinamen, and she could hear them from where she stood, taking their early morning breakfast. Below their dining room was her husband's grocery store. Across the way was a large restaurant. Last night it had been resplendent with gay colored lanterns and the sound of music. The rejoicings over "the completion of the moon," by Quong Sum's firstborn, had been long and loud, and had caused her to tie a handkerchief over her ears. She, a bereaved mother, had it not in her heart to rejoice with other parents. This morning the place was more in accord with her mood. It was still and quiet. The revelers had dispersed or were asleep.

A roly-poly woman in black sateen, with long pendant earrings in her ears, looked up from the street below and waved her a smiling greeting. It was her old neighbor, Kuie Hoe, the wife of the gold embosser, Mark Sing. With her was a little boy in yellow jacket and lavender pantaloons. Lae Choo remembered him as a baby. She used to like to play with him in those days when she had no child of her own. What a long time ago that seemed! She caught her breath in a sigh, and laughed instead.

"Why are you so merry?" called her husband from within.

"Because my Little One is coming home," answered Lae Choo. "I am a happy mother—a happy mother."

She pattered into the room with a smile on her face.

—

The noon hour had arrived. The rice was steaming in the bowls and a fragrant dish of chicken and bamboo shoots was awaiting Hom Hing. Not for one moment had Lae Choo paused to rest during the morning hours; her activity had been ceaseless. Every now and again, however, she had raised her eyes to the gilded clock on the curiously carved mantelpiece. Once, she had exclaimed:

"Why so long, oh! why so long?" Then apostrophizing herself: "Lae Choo, be happy. The Little One is coming! The Little One is coming!" Several times she burst into tears and several times she laughed aloud.

Hom Hing entered the room; his arms hung down by his side.

"The Little One!" shrieked Lae Choo.

"They bid me call tomorrow."

With a moan the mother sank to the floor.

The noon hour passed. The dinner remained on the table.

III

The winter rains were over: the spring had come to California, flushing the hills with green and causing an ever-changing pageant of flowers to pass over them. But there was no spring in Lae Choo's heart, for the Little One remained away from her arms. He was being kept in a mission. White women were caring for him, and though for one full moon he had pined for his mother and refused to be comforted he was now apparently happy and contented. Five moons or five months had gone by since the day he had passed with Lae Choo through the Golden Gate; but the great Government at Washington still delayed sending the answer which would return him to his parents.

———

Hom Hing was disconsolately rolling up and down the balls in his abacus box when a keen-faced young man stepped into his store.

"What news?" asked the Chinese merchant.

"This!" The young man brought forth a typewritten letter. Hom Hing read the words:

"Re Chinese child, alleged to be the son of Hom Hing, Chinese merchant, doing business at 425 Clay Street, San Francisco.

"Same will have attention as soon as possible."

Hom Hing returned the letter, and without a word continued his manipulation of the counting machine.

"Have you anything to say?" asked the young man.

"Nothing. They have sent the same letter fifteen times before. Have you not yourself showed it to me?"

"True!" The young man eyed the Chinese merchant furtively. He had a proposition to make and he was pondering whether or not the time was opportune.

"How is your wife?" he inquired solicitously—and diplomatically.

Hom Hing shook his head mournfully.

"She seems less every day," he replied. "Her food she takes only when I bid her and her tears fall continually. She finds no pleasure in dress or flowers and cares not to see her friends. Her eyes stare all night. I think before another moon she will pass into the land of spirits."

"No!" exclaimed the young man, genuinely startled.

"If the boy not come home I lose my wife sure," continued Hom Hing with bitter sadness.

"It's not right," cried the young man indignantly. Then he made his proposition.

The Chinese father's eyes brightened exceedingly.

"Will I like you to go to Washington and make them give you the paper to restore my son?" cried he. "How can you ask when you know my heart's desire?"

"Then," said the young fellow, "I will start next week. I am anxious to see this thing through if only for the sake of your wife's peace of mind."

"I will call her. To hear what you think to do will make her glad," said Hom Hing.

He called a message to Lae Choo upstairs through a tube in the wall.

In a few moments she appeared, listless, wan, and hollow-eyed; but when her husband told her the young lawyer's suggestion she became as one electrified; her form straightened, her eyes glistened; the color flushed to her cheeks.

"Oh," she cried, turning to James Clancy, "you are a hundred man good!"

The young man felt somewhat embarrassed; his eyes shifted a little under the intense gaze of the Chinese mother.

"Well, we must get your boy for you," he responded. "Of course"—turning to Hom Hing—"it will cost a little money. You can't get fellows to hurry the Government for you without gold in your pocket."

Hom Hing stared blankly for a moment. Then: "How much do you want, Mr. Clancy?" he asked quietly.

"Well, I will need at least five hundred to start with."

Hom Hing cleared his throat.

"I think I told to you the time I last paid you for writing letters for me and seeing the Custom boss here that nearly all I had was gone!"

"Oh, well then we won't talk about it, old fellow. It won't harm the boy to stay where he is, and your wife may get over it all right."

"What that you say?" quavered Lae Choo.

James Clancy looked out of the window.

"He says," explained Hom Hing in English, "that to get our boy we have to have much money."

"Money! Oh, yes."

Lae Choo nodded her head.

"I have not got the money to give him."

For a moment Lae Choo gazed wonderingly from one face to the other; then, comprehension dawning upon her, with swift anger, pointing to the lawyer, she cried: "You not one hundred man good; you just common white man."

"Yes, ma'am," returned James Clancy, bowing and smiling ironically.

Hom Hing pushed his wife behind him and addressed the lawyer again: "I might try," said he, "to raise something; but five hundred—it is not possible."

"What about four?"

"I tell you I have next to nothing left and my friends are not rich."

"Very well!"

The lawyer moved leisurely toward the door, pausing on its threshold to light a cigarette.

"Stop, white man; white man, stop!"

Lae Choo, panting and terrified, had started forward and now stood beside him, clutching his sleeve excitedly.

"You say you can go to get paper to bring my Little One to me if Hom Hing give you five hundred dollars?"

The lawyer nodded carelessly; his eyes were intent upon the cigarette which would not take the fire from the match.

"Then you go get paper. If Hom Hing not can give you five hundred dollars—I give you perhaps what more that much."

She slipped a heavy gold bracelet from her wrist and held it out to the man. Mechanically he took it.

"I go get more!"

She scurried away, disappearing behind the door through which she had come.

"Oh, look here, I can't accept this," said James Clancy, walking back to Hom Hing and laying down the bracelet before him.

"It's all right," said Hom Hing, seriously, "pure China gold. My wife's parent give it to her when we married."

"But I can't take it anyway," protested the young man.

"It is all same as money. And you want money to go to Washington," replied Hom Hing in a matter of fact manner.

"See, my jade earrings—my gold buttons—my hairpins—my comb of pearl and my rings—one, two, three, four, five rings; very good—very good—all same much money. I give them all to you. You take and bring me paper for my Little One."

Lae Choo piled up her jewels before the lawyer.

Hom Hing laid a restraining hand upon her shoulder. "Not all, my wife," he said in Chinese. He selected a ring—his gift to Lae Choo when she dreamed of the tree with the red flower. The rest of the jewels he pushed toward the white man.

"Take them and sell them," said he. "They will pay your fare to Washington and bring you back with the paper."

For one moment James Clancy hesitated. He was not a sentimental man; but something within him arose against accepting such payment for his services.

"They are good, good," pleadingly asserted Lae Choo, seeing his hesitation.

Whereupon he seized the jewels, thrust them into his coat pocket, and walked rapidly away from the store.

IV

Lae Choo followed after the missionary woman through the mission nursery school. Her heart was beating so high with happiness that she could scarcely breathe. The paper had come at last—the precious paper which gave Hom Hing and his wife the right to the possession of their own child. It was ten months now since he had been taken from them—ten months since the sun had ceased to shine for Lae Choo.

The room was filled with children—most of them wee tots, but none so wee as her own. The mission woman talked as she walked. She told Lae Choo that little Kim, as he had been named by the school, was the pet of the place, and that his little tricks and ways amused and delighted everyone. He had been rather difficult to manage at first and had cried much for his mother; "but children so soon forget, and after a month he seemed quite at home and played around as bright and happy as a bird."

"Yes," responded Lae Choo. "Oh, yes, yes!"

But she did not hear what was said to her. She was walking in a maze of anticipatory joy.

"Wait here, please," said the mission woman, placing Lae Choo in a chair. "The very youngest ones are having their breakfast."

She withdrew for a moment—it seemed like an hour to the mother—then she reappeared leading by the hand a little boy dressed in blue cotton overalls and white-soled shoes. The little boy's face was round and dimpled and his eyes were very bright.

"Little One, ah, my Little One!" cried Lae Choo.

She fell on her knees and stretched her hungry arms toward her son.

But the Little One shrunk from her and tried to hide himself in the folds of the white woman's skirt.

"Go'way, go'way!" he bade his mother.

THE CHINESE LILY

Mermei lived in an upstairs room of a Chinatown dwelling-house. There were other little Chinese women living on the same floor, but Mermei never went amongst them. She was not as they were. She was a cripple. A fall had twisted her legs so that she moved around with difficulty and scarred her face so terribly that none save Lin John cared to look upon it. Lin John, her brother, was a laundryman, working for another of his countrymen. Lin John and Mermei had come to San Francisco with their parents when they were small children. Their mother had died the day she entered the foreign city, and the father the week following, both having contracted a fever on the steamer. Mermei and Lin John were then taken in charge by their father's brother, and although he was a poor man he did his best for them until called away by death.

Long before her uncle died Mermei had met with the accident that had made her not as other girls; but that had only strengthened her brother's affection, and old Lin Wan died happy in the knowledge that Lin John would ever put Mermei before himself.

So Mermei lived in her little upstairs room, cared for by Lin John, and scarcely an evening passed that he did not call to see her. One evening, however, Lin John failed to appear, and Mermei began to feel very sad and lonely. Mermei could embroider all day in contented silence if she knew that in the evening someone would come to whom she could communicate all the thoughts that filled a small black head that knew nothing of life save what it saw from an upstairs window. Mermei's window looked down upon the street, and she would sit for hours, pressed close against it, watching those who passed below and all that took place. That day she had seen many things which she had put into her mental portfolio for Lin John's edification when evening should come. Two yellow-robed priests had passed below on their way to the joss house in the next street; a little bird with a white breast had fluttered against the window-pane; a man carrying an image of a Gambling Cash Tiger had entered the house across the street; and six young girls of about her own age, dressed gaily as if to attend a wedding, had also passed over the same threshold.

But when nine o'clock came and no Lin John, the girl began to cry softly. She did not often shed tears, but for some reason unknown to Mermei herself, the sight of those joyous girls caused sad reflections. In the midst of her weeping a timid knock was heard. It was not Lin John. He always gave a loud rap, then entered without waiting to be bidden. Mermei hobbled to the door, pulled it open, and there, in the dim light of the hall without, beheld a young girl—the most beautiful young girl that Mermei had ever seen—and she stood there extending to Mermei a blossom from a Chinese lily plant. Mermei understood the meaning of the offered flower, and accepting it, beckoned for her visitor to follow her into her room.

What a delightful hour that was to Mermei! She forgot that she was scarred and crippled, and she and the young girl chattered out their little hearts to one another. "Lin John is dear, but one can't talk to a man, even if he is a brother, as one can to one the same as one-self," said Mermei to Sin Far—her new friend, and Sin Far, the meaning of whose name was Pure Flower, or Chinese Lily, answered:

"Yes, indeed. The woman must be the friend of the woman, and the man the friend of the man. Is it not so in the country that Heaven loves?"

"What beneficent spirit moved you to come to my door?" asked Mermei.

"I know not," replied Sin Far, "save that I was lonely. We have but lately moved here, my sister, my sister's husband, and myself. My sister is a bride, and there is much to say between her and her husband. Therefore, in the evening, when the day's duties are done, I am alone. Several times, hearing that you were sick, I ventured to your door; but failed to knock, because always when I drew near, I heard the voice of him whom they call your brother. Tonight, as I returned from an errand for my sister, I heard only the sound of weeping—so I hastened to my room and plucked the lily for you."

The next evening when Lin John explained how he had been obliged to work the evening before Mermei answered brightly that that was all right. She loved him just as much as ever and was just as glad to see him as ever; but if work prevented him from calling he was not to worry. She had found a friend who would cheer her loneliness.

Lin John was surprised, but glad to hear such news, and it came to pass that when he beheld Sin Far, her sweet and gentle face, her pretty drooped eyelids and arched eyebrows, he began to think of apple and peach and plum trees showering their dainty blossoms in the country that Heaven loves.

—

It was about four o'clock in the afternoon. Lin John, working in his laundry, paid little attention to the street uproar and the clang of the engines rushing by. He had no thought of what it meant to him and would have continued at his work undisturbed had not a boy put his head into the door and shouted:

"Lin John, the house in which your sister lives is on fire!"

The tall building was in flames when Lin John reached it. The uprising tongues licked his face as he sprung up the ladder no other man dared ascend.

"I will not go. It is best for me to die," and Mermei resisted her friend with all her puny strength.

"The ladder will not bear the weight of both of us. You are his sister," calmly replied Sin Far.

"But he loves you best. You and he can be happy together. I am not fit to live."

"May Lin John decide, Mermei?"

"Yes, Lin John may decide."

Lin John reached the casement. For one awful second he wavered. Then his eyes sought the eyes of his sister's friend.

"Come, Mermei," he called.

———

"Where is Sin Far?" asked Mermei when she became conscious.

"Sin Far is in the land of happy spirits."

"And I am still in this sad, dark world."

"Speak not so, little one. Your brother loves you and will protect you from the darkness."

"But you loved Sin Far better—and she loved you."

Lin John bowed his head.

"Alas!" wept Mermei. "That I should live to make others sad!"

"Nay," said Lin John, "Sin Far is happy. And I—I did my duty with her approval, aye, at her bidding. How then, little sister, can I be sad?"

THE SMUGGLING OF TIE CO

Amongst the daring men who engage in contrabanding Chinese from Canada into the United States Jack Fabian ranks as the boldest in deed, the cleverest in scheming, and the most successful in outwitting Government officers.

Uncommonly strong in person, tall and well built, with fine features and a pair of keen, steady blue eyes, gifted with a sort of rough eloquence and of much personal fascination, it is no wonder that we fellows regard him as our chief and are bound to follow where he leads. With Fabian at our head we engage in the wildest adventures and find such places of concealment for our human goods as none but those who take part in a desperate business would dare to dream of.

Jack, however, is not in search of glory—money is his object. One day when a romantic friend remarked that it was very kind of him to help the poor Chinamen over the border, a cynical smile curled his moustache.

"Kind!" he echoed. "Well, I haven't yet had time to become sentimental over the matter. It is merely a matter of dollars and cents, though, of course, to a man of my strict principles, there is a certain pleasure to be derived from getting ahead of the Government. A poor devil does now and then like to take a little out of those millionaire concerns."

It was last summer and Fabian was somewhat down on his luck. A few months previously, to the surprise of us all, he had made a blunder, which resulted in his capture by American officers, and he and his companion, together with five uncustomed Chinamen, had been lodged in a county jail to await trial.

But loafing behind bars did not agree with Fabian's energetic nature, so one dark night, by means of a saw which had been given to him by a very innocent-looking visitor the day before, he made good his escape, and after a long, hungry, detective-hunted tramp through woods and bushes, found himself safe in Canada.

He had had a three months' sojourn in prison, and during that time some changes had taken place in smuggling circles. Some ingenious lawyers had devised a scheme by which any young Chinaman on payment of a couple of hundred dollars could procure a father, which father, would swear the young Chinaman was born in America—thus proving him to be an American citizen with the right to breathe United States air. And the Chinese themselves, assisted by some white men, were manufacturing certificates establishing their right to cross the border, and in that way were crossing over in large batches.

That sort of trick naturally spoiled our fellows' business, but we all know that "Yankee sharper" games can hold good only for a short while; so we bided our time and waited in patience.

Not so Fabian. He became very restless and wandered around with glowering looks. He was sitting one day in a laundry, the proprietor of which had sent out many a boy through our chief's instrumentality. Indeed, Fabian is said to have "rushed over" to "Uncle Sam" himself some five hundred Celestials, and if Fabian had not been an exceedingly generous fellow he might now be a gentleman of leisure instead of an unimmortalized Rob Roy.

Well, Fabian was sitting in the laundry of Chen Ting Lung & Co., telling a nice-looking young Chinaman that he was so broke that he'd be willing to take over even one man at a time.

The young Chinaman looked thoughtfully into Fabian's face. "Would you take me?" he inquired.

"Take you!" echoed Fabian. "Why, you are one of the 'bosses' here. You don't mean to say that you are hankering after a place where it would take you years to get as high up in the 'washee, washee' business as you are now?"

"Yes, I want go," replied Tie Co. "I want go to New York and I will pay you fifty dollars and all expense if you take me, and not say you take me to my partners."

"There's no accounting for a Chinaman," muttered Fabian; but he gladly agreed to the proposal and a night was fixed.

"What is the name of the firm you are going to?" inquired the white man.

Chinamen who intend being smuggled always make arrangements with some Chinese firm in the States to receive them.

Tie Co hesitated, then mumbled something which sounded like "Quong Wo Yuen" or "Long Lo Toon," Fabian was not sure which, but did not repeat the question, not being sufficiently interested.

He left the laundry, nodding goodbye to Tie Co as he passed outside the window, and the Chinaman nodded back, a faint smile on his small, delicate face lingering until Fabian's receding form was lost to view.

It was a pleasant night on which the two men set out. Fabian had a rig waiting at the corner of the street; Tie Co, dressed in citizen's clothes, stepped into it unobserved, and the smuggler and would-be-smuggled were soon out of the city. They had a merry drive, for Fabian's liking for Tie Co was very real; he had known him for several years, and the lad's quick intelligence interested him.

The second day they left their horse at a farmhouse, where Fabian would call for it on his return trip, crossed a river in a rowboat before the sun was up, and plunged into a wood in which they would remain till evening. It was raining, but through mud and wind and rain they trudged slowly and heavily.

Tie Co paused now and then to take breath. Once Fabian remarked:

"You are not a very strong lad, Tie Co. It's a pity you have to work as you do for your living," and Tie Co had answered:

"Work velly good! No work, Tie Co die."

Fabian looked at the lad protectingly, wondering in a careless way why this Chinaman seemed to him so different from the others.

"Wouldn't you like to be back in China?" he asked.

"No," said Tie Co decidedly.

"Why?"

"I not know why," answered Tie Co.

Fabian laughed.

"Haven't you got a nice little wife, at home?" he continued. "I hear you people marry very young."

"No, I no wife," asserted his companion with à choky little laugh. "I never have no wife."

"Nonsense," joked Fabian. "Why, Tie Co, think how nice it would be to have a little woman cook your rice and to love you."

"I not have wife," repeated Tie Co seriously. "I not like woman, I like man."

"You confirmed old bachelor!" ejaculated Fabian.

"I like you," said Tie Co, his boyish voice sounding clear and sweet in the wet woods. "I like you so much that I want go to New York, so you make fifty dollars. I no flend in New York."

"What!" exclaimed Fabian.

"Oh, I solly I tell you, Tie Co velly solly," and the Chinese boy shuffled on with bowed head.

"Look here, Tie Co," said Fabian; "I won't have you do this for my sake. You have been very foolish, and I don't care for your fifty dollars. I do not need it half as much as you do. Good God! how ashamed you make me feel—I who have blown in my thousands in idle pleasures cannot take the little you have slaved for. We are in New York State now. When we get out of this wood we will have to walk over a bridge which crosses a river. On the other side, not far from where we cross, there is a railway station. Instead of buying you a ticket for the city of New York I shall take a train with you for Toronto."

Tie Co did not answer—he seemed to be thinking deeply. Suddenly he pointed to where some fallen trees lay.

"Two men run away behind there," cried he.

Fabian looked round them anxiously; his keen eyes seemed to pierce the gloom in his endeavor to catch a glimpse of any person; but no man was visible, and, save the dismal sighing of the wind among the trees, all was quiet.

"There's no one," he said somewhat gruffly—he was rather startled, for they were a mile over the border and he knew that the Government officers were on a sharp lookout for him, and felt, despite his strength, if any trick or surprise were attempted it would go hard with him.

"If they catch you with me it be too bad," sententiously remarked Tie Co. It seemed as if his words were in answer to Fabian's thoughts.

"But they will not catch us; so cheer up your heart, my boy," replied the latter, more heartily than he felt.

"If they come, and I not with you, they not take you and it be all lite."

"Yes," assented Fabian, wondering what his companion was thinking about.

They emerged from the woods in the dusk of the evening and were soon on the bridge crossing the river. When they were near the center Tie Co stopped and looked into Fabian's face.

"Man come for you, I not here, man no hurt you." And with the words he whirled like a flash over the rail.

In another flash Fabian was after him. But though a first-class swimmer, the white man's efforts were of no avail, and Tie Co was borne away from him by the swift current.

Cold and dripping wet, Fabian dragged himself up the bank and found himself a prisoner.

"So your Chinaman threw himself into the river. What was that for?" asked one of the Government officers.

"I think he was out of his head," replied Fabian. And he fully believed what he uttered.

"We tracked you right through the woods," said another of the captors. "We thought once the boy caught sight of us."

Fabian remained silent.

———

Tie Co's body was picked up the next day. Tie Co's body, and yet not Tie Co, for Tie Co was a youth, and the body found with Tie Co's face and dressed in Tie Co's clothes was the body of a girl—a woman.

Nobody in the laundry of Chen Ting Lung & Co.—no Chinaman in Canada or New York—could explain the mystery. Tie Co had come out to Canada with a number of other youths. Though not very strong he had always been a good worker and "very smart." He had been quiet and reserved among his own countrymen; had refused to smoke tobacco or opium, and had been a regular attendant at Sunday schools and a great favorite with Mission ladies.

Fabian was released in less than a week. "No evidence against him," said the Commissioner, who was not aware that the prisoner was the man who had broken out of jail but a month before.

Fabian is now very busy; there are lots of boys taking his helping hand over the border, but none of them are like Tie Co; and sometimes, between whiles, Fabian finds himself pondering long and earnestly over the mystery of Tie Co's life—and death.

THE GOD OF RESTORATION

"He that hath wine hath many friends," muttered Koan-lo the Second, as he glanced backward into the store out of which he was stepping. It was a Chinese general store, well stocked with all manner of quaint wares, and about a dozen Chinamen were sitting around; whilst in an adjoining room could be seen the recumbent forms of several smokers who were discussing business and indulging in the fascinating pipe during the intervals of conversation.

Noticeable amongst the smokers was Koan-lo the First, a tall, middle-aged Chinaman, wearing a black cap with a red button. Koan-lo the First was cousin to Koan-lo the Second, but whereas Koan-lo the Second was young and penniless, Koan-lo the First was one of the wealthiest Chinese merchants in San Francisco and a mighty man amongst the people of his name in that city, who regarded him as a father.

Koan-lo the Second had been instructed by Koan-lo the First to meet Sie, the latter's bride, who was arriving that day by steamer from China. Koan-lo the First was too busy a man to go down himself to the docks.

So Koan-lo the Second and Sie met—though not for the first time. Five years before in a suburb of Canton City they had said to one another: "I love you."

Koan-lo the Second was an orphan and had been educated and cared for from youth upward by Koan-lo the First.

Sie was the daughter of a slave, which will explain why she and Koan-lo the Second had had the opportunity to know one another before the latter left with his cousin for America. In China the daughters of slaves are allowed far more liberty than girls belonging to a higher class of society.

"Koan-lo, ah, Koan-lo," cooed Sie softly and happily as she recognized her lover.

"Sie, my sweetest heart," returned Koan-lo the Second, his voice both glad and sad.

He saw that a mistake had been made—that Sie believed that the man who was to be her husband was himself—Koan-lo the Second.

And all the love that was in him awoke, and he became dizzy thinking of what might yet be.

Could he explain that the Koan-lo who had purchased Sie for his bride, and to whom she of right belonged, was his cousin and not himself? Could he deliver to the Koan-lo who had many friends and stores of precious valuables the only friend, the only treasure he had ever possessed? And was it likely that Sie would be happy eating the rice of Koan-lo the First when she loved him, Koan-lo the Second?

Sie's little fingers crept into his. She leaned against him. "I am tired. Shall we soon rest?" said she.

"Yes, very soon, my Sie," he murmured, putting his arm around her.

"I was too glad when my father told me that you had sent for me," she whispered. "I said: 'How good of Koan-lo to remember me all these years.'"

"And did you not remember me, my jess'-mine flower?"

"Why need you ask? You know the days and nights have been filled with you."

"Having remembered me, why should you have dreamt that I might have forgotten you?"

"There is a difference. You are a man; I am a woman."

"You have been mine now for over two weeks," said Koan-lo the Second. "Do you still love me, Sie?"

"Look into mine eyes and see," she answered.

"And are you happy?"

"Happy! Yes, and this is the happiest day of all, because today my father obtains his freedom."

"How is that, Sie?"

"Why, Koan-lo, you know. Does not my father receive today the balance of the price you pay for me, and is not that, added to what you sent in advance, sufficient to purchase my father's freedom? My dear, good father—he has worked so hard all these years. He has ever been so kind to me. How glad am I to think that through me the God of Restoration has decreed that he shall no longer be a slave. Yes, I am the happiest woman in the world today."

Sie kissed her husband's hand.

He drew it away and hid with it his face.

"Ah, dear husband!" cried Sie. "You are very sick."

"No, not sick," replied the miserable Koan-lo—"but, Sie, I must tell you that I am a very poor man, and we have got to leave this pretty house in the country and go to some city where I will have to work hard and you will scarcely have enough to eat."

"Kind, generous Koan-lo," answered Sie, "you have ruined yourself for my sake; you paid too high a price for me. Ah, unhappy Sie, who has pulled Koan-lo into the dust! Now let me be your servant, for gladly would I starve for your sake. I care for Koan-lo, not riches."

And she fell on her knees before the young man, who raised her gently, saying:

"Sie, I am, unworthy of such devotion, and your words drive a thousand spears into my heart. Hear my confession. I am your husband, but I am not the man who bought you. My cousin, Koan-lo the First, sent for you to come from China. It was he who bargained for you, and paid half the price your father asked whilst you were in Canton, and agreed to pay the balance upon sight of your face. Alas! the balance will never be paid, for as I have stolen you from my cousin, he is not bound to keep to the agreement, and your father is still a slave."

Sie stood motionless, overwhelmed by the sudden and terrible news. She looked at her husband bewilderedly.

"Is it true, Koan-lo? Must my father remain a slave?" she asked.

"Yes, it is true," replied her husband. "But we have still one another, and you say you care not for poverty. So forgive me and forget your father. I forgot all for love of you."

He attempted to draw her to him, but with a pitiful cry she turned and fled.

—

Koan-lo the First sat smoking and meditating.

Many moons had gone by since Koan-lo the Second had betrayed the trust of Koan-lo the First, and Koan-lo the First was wondering what Koan-lo the Second was doing, and how he was living. "He had little money and was unused to working hard, and with a woman to support what will the dog do?" thought the old man. He felt injured and bitter, but toward the evening, after long smoking, his heart became softened, and he said to his pipe: "Well, well, he had a loving feeling for her, and the young I suppose must mate with the young. I think I could overlook his ungratefulness were he to come and seek forgiveness."

"Great and honored sir, the dishonored Sie kneels before you and begs you to put your foot on her head."

These words were uttered by a young Chinese girl of rare beauty who had entered the room suddenly and prostrated herself before Koan-lo the First. He looked up angrily.

"Ah, I see the false woman who made her father a liar!" he cried.

Tears fell from the downcast eyes of Sie, the kneeler.

"Good sir," said she, "ere I had become a woman or your cousin a man, we loved one another, and when we met after a long separation, we both forgot our duty. But the God of Restoration worked with my heart. I repented and now am come to you to give myself up to be your slave, to work for you until the flesh drops from my bones, if such be your desire, only asking that you will send to my father the balance of my purchase price, for he is too old and feeble to be a slave. Sir, you are known to be a more than just man. Oh, grant my request! 'Tis for my father's sake I plead. For many years he nourished me, with trouble and care; and my heart almost breaks when I think of him. Punish me for my misdeeds, dress me in rags, and feed me on the meanest food! Only let me serve you and make myself of use to you, so that I may be worth my father's freedom."

"And what of my cousin? Are you now false to him?"

"No, not false to Koan-lo, my husband—only true to my father."

"And you wish me, whom you have injured, to free your father?"

Sie's head dropped lower as she replied:

"I wish to be your slave. I wish to pay with the labor of my hands the debt I owe you and the debt I owe my father. For this I have left my husband."

Koan-lo the First arose, lifted Sie's chin with his hand, and contemplated with earnest eyes her face.

"Your heart is not all bad," he observed. "Sit down and listen. I will not buy you for my slave, for in this country it is against the law to buy a woman for a slave; but I will hire you for five years to be my servant, and for that time you will do my bidding, and after that you will be free. Rest in peace concerning your father."

"May the sun ever shine on you, most gracious master!" cried Sie.

Then Koan-lo the First pointed out to her a hallway leading to a little room, which room he said she could have for her own private use while she remained with him.

Sie thanked him and was leaving his presence when the door was burst open and Koan-lo the Second, looking haggard and wild, entered. He rushed up to Sie and clutched her by the shoulder.

"You are mine!" he shouted. "I will kill you before you become another man's!"

"Cousin," said Koan-lo the First, "I wish not to have the woman to be my wife, but I claim her as my servant. She has already received her wages—her father's freedom."

Koan-lo the Second gazed bewilderedly into the faces of his wife and cousin. Then he threw up his hands and cried:

"Oh, Koan-lo, my cousin, I have been evil. Always have I envied you and carried bitter thoughts of you in my heart. Even your kindness to me in the past has provoked my ill will, and when I have seen you surrounded by friends, I have said scornfully: 'He that hath wine hath many friends,' although I well knew the people loved you for your good heart. And Sie I have deceived. I took her to myself, knowing that she thought I was what I was not. I caused her to believe she was mine by all rights."

"So I am yours," broke in Sie tremblingly.

"So she shall be yours—when you are worthy of such a pearl and can guard and keep it," said Koan-lo the First. Then waving his cousin away from Sie, he continued:

"This is your punishment; the God of Restoration demands it. For five years you shall not see the face of Sie, your wife. Meanwhile, study, think, be honest, and work."

———

"Your husband comes for you today. Does the thought make you glad?" questioned Koan-lo the First.

Sie smiled and blushed.

"I shall be sorry to leave you," she replied.

"But more glad than sad," said the old man. "Sie, your husband is now a fine fellow. He has changed wonderfully during his years of probation."

"Then I shall neither know nor love him," said Sie mischievously. "Why, here he—"

"My sweet one!"

"My husband!"

"My children, take my blessing; be good and be happy. I go to my pipe, to dream of bliss if not to find it."

With these words Koan-lo the First retired.

"Is he not almost as a god?" said Sie.

"Yes," answered her husband, drawing her onto his knee. "He has been better to me than I have deserved. And you—ah, Sie, how can you care for me when you know what a bad fellow I have been?"

"Well," said Sie contentedly, "it is always our best friends who know how bad we are."

THE THREE SOULS OF AH SO NAN

I

The sun was conquering the morning fog, dappling with gold the gray waters of San Francisco's bay, and throwing an emerald radiance over the islands around.

Close to the long line of wharves lay motionless brigs and schooners, while farther off in the harbor were ships of many nations riding at anchor.

A fishing fleet was steering in from the open sea, scudding before the wind like a flock of seabirds. All night long had the fishers toiled in the deep. Now they were returning with the results of their labor.

A young Chinese girl, watching the fleet from the beach of Fisherman's Cove, shivered in the morning air. Over her blue cotton blouse she wore no wrap; on her head, no covering. All her interest was centered in one lone boat which lagged behind the rest, being heavier freighted. The fisherman was of her own race. When his boat was beached he sprang to her side.

"O'Yam, what brings you here?" he questioned low, for the curious eyes of his fellow fishermen were on her.

"Your mother is dying," she answered.

The young man spake a few words in English to a Greek whose boat lay alongside his. The Greek answered in the same tongue. Then Fou Wang threw down his nets and, with the girl following, walked quickly along the waterfront, past the wharves, the warehouses, and the grogshops, up a zigzag hill and into the heart of

Chinatown. Neither spoke until they reached their destination, a dingy three-storied building.

The young man began to ascend the stairs, the girl to follow. Fou Wang looked back and shook his head. The girl paused on the lowest step.

"May I not come?" she pleaded.

"Today is for sorrow," returned Fou Wang.

"I would, for a time, forget all that belongs to the joy of life."

The girl threw her sleeve over her head and backed out of the open door.

"What is the matter?" inquired a kind voice, and a woman laid her hand upon her shoulder.

O'Yam's bosom heaved.

"Oh, Liuchi," she cried, "the mother of Fou Wang is dying, and you know what that means to me."

The woman eyed her compassionately.

"Your father, I know," said she, as she unlocked a door and led her companion into a room opening on to the street, "has long wished for an excuse to set at naught your betrothal to Fou Wang; but I am sure the lad to whom you are both sun and moon will never give him one."

She offered O'Yam some tea, but the girl pushed it aside. "You know not Fou Wang," she replied, sadly yet proudly. "He will follow his conscience, though he lose the sun, the moon, and the whole world."

A young woman thrust her head through the door.

"The mother of Fou Wang is dead," cried she.

—

"She was a good woman—a kind and loving mother," said Liuchi, as she gazed down upon the still features of her friend.

The young daughter of Ah So Nan burst into fresh weeping. Her pretty face was much swollen. Ah So Nan had been well loved by her children, and the falling tears were not merely waters of ceremony.

At the foot of the couch upon which the dead was laid, stood Fou

Wang, his face stern and immovable, his eye solemn, yet luminous with a steadfast fire. Over his head was thrown a white cloth. From morn till eve had he stood thus, contemplating the serene countenance of his mother and vowing that nothing should be left undone which could be done to prove his filial affection and desire to comfort her spirit in the land to which it had flown. "Three years, O mother, will I give to thee and grief. Three years will I minister to thy three souls," he vowed within himself, remembering how sacred to the dead woman were the customs and observances of her own country. They were also sacred to him. Living in America, in the midst of Americans and Americanized Chinese, the family of Fou Wang, with the exception of one, had clung tenaciously to the beliefs of their forefathers.

"All the living must die, and dying, return to the ground. The limbs and the flesh moulder away below, and hidden away, become the earth of the fields; but the spirit issues forth and is displayed on high in a condition of glorious brightness," quoted a yellow-robed priest, swinging an incense burner before a small candle-lighted altar.

It was midnight when the mourning friends of the family of Fou Wang left the chief mourner alone with his dead mother.

His sister, Fin Fan, and the girl who was his betrothed wife brushed his garments as they passed him by. The latter timidly touched his hand—an involuntary act of sympathy—but if he were conscious of that sympathy, he paid no heed to it, and his gaze never wavered from the face of the dead.

II

"My girl, Moy Ding Fong is ready if Fou Wang is not, and you must marry this year. I have sworn you shall."

Kien Lung walked out of the room with a determined step. He was an Americanized Chinese and had little regard for what he derided as "the antiquated customs of China," save when it was to his interest to follow them. He was also a widower desirous of marrying again, but undesirous of having two women of like years, one his wife, the other his daughter, under the same roof-tree.

Left alone, O'Yam's thoughts became sorrowful, almost despairing. Six moons had gone by since Ah So Nan had passed away, yet the son of Ah So Nan had not once, during that time, spoken one word to his betrothed wife. Occasionally she had passed him on the street; but always he had gone by with uplifted countenance, and in his eyes the beauty of piety and peace. At least, so it seemed to the girl, and the thought of marriage with him had seemed almost sacrilegious. But now it had come to this. If Fou Wang adhered to his resolve to mourn three years for his mother, what would become of her? She thought of old Moy Ding Fong and shuddered. It was bitter, bitter.

There was a rapping at the door. A young girl lifted the latch and stepped in. It was Fin Fan, the sister of her betrothed.

"I have brought my embroidery work," said she, "I thought we could have a little talk before sundown when I must away to prepare the evening meal."

O'Yam, who was glad to see her visitor, brewed some fresh tea and settled down for an exchange of confidences.

"I am not going to abide by it," said Fin Fan at last. "Hom Hing is obliged to return to China two weeks hence, and with or without Fou Wang's consent I go with the man to whom my mother betrothed me."

"Without Fou Wang's consent!" echoed O'Yam.

"Yes," returned Fin Fan, snapping off a thread. "Without my honorable brother's consent."

"And your mother gone but six moons!"

O'Yam's face wore a shocked expression.

"Does the fallen leaf grieve because the green one remains on the tree?" queried Fin Fan.

"You must love Hom Hing well," murmured O'Yam—"more than Fou Wang loves me."

"Nay," returned her companion, "Fou Wang's love for you is as big as mine for Hom Hing. It is my brother's conscience alone that stands between him and you. You know that."

"He loves not me," sighed O'Yam.

"If he does not love you," returned Fin Fan, "why, when we heard that you were unwell, did he sleeplessly pace his room night after night until the news came that you were restored to health? Why does he treasure a broken fan you have cast aside?"

"Ah, well!" smiled O'Yam.

Fin Fan laughed softly.

"Fou Wang is not as other men," said she. "His conscience is an inheritance from his great-great-grandfather." Her face became pensive as she added: "It is sad to go across the sea without an elder brother's blessing."

She repeated this to Liuchi and Mai Gwi Far, the widow, whom she met on her way home.

"Why should you," inquired the latter, "when there is a way by which to obtain it?"

"How?"

"Did Ah So Nan leave no garments behind her—such garments as would well fit her three souls—and is it not always easy to delude the serious and the wise?"

"Ah!"

III

O'Yam climbed the stairs to the joss house. The desire for solitude brought her there; but when she had closed the door upon herself, she found that she was not alone. Fou Wang was there. Before the images of the Three Wise Ones he stood, silent, motionless.

"He is communing with his mother's spirit," thought O'Yam. She beheld him through a mist of tears. Love filled her whole being. She dared not move, because she was afraid he would turn and see her, and then, of course, he would go away. She would stay near him for a few moments and then retire.

The dim light of the place, the quietness in the midst of noise, the fragrance of some burning incense, soothed and calmed her. It was as if all the sorrow and despair that had overwhelmed her when her father had told her to prepare for her wedding with Moy Ding Fong had passed away.

After a few moments she stepped back softly toward the door. But she was too late. Fou Wang turned and beheld her.

She fluttered like a bird until she saw that, surprised by her presence, he had forgotten death and thought only of life—of life and love. A glad, eager light shone in his eyes. He made a swift step toward her. Then—he covered his face with his hands.

"Fou Wang!" cried O'Yam, love at last overcoming superstition. "Must I become the wife of Moy Ding Fong?"

"No, ah, no!" he moaned.

"Then," said the girl in desperation, "take me to yourself."

Fou Wang's hands fell to his side. For a moment he looked into that pleading face—and wavered.

A little bird flew in through an open window, and perching itself upon an altar, began twittering.

Fou Wang started back, the expression on his face changing.

"A warning from the dead," he muttered, "a warning from the dead!"

An iron hand gripped O'Yam's heart. Life itself seemed to have closed upon her.

IV

It was afternoon before evening, and the fog was rolling in from the sea. Quietness reigned in the plot of ground sacred to San Francisco's Chinese dead when Fou Wang deposited a bundle at the foot of his mother's grave and prepared for the ceremony of ministering to her three souls.

The fragrance from a wall of fir trees nearby stole to his nostrils as he cleared the weeds and withered leaves from his parent's resting place. As he placed the bowls of rice and chicken and the vase of incense where he was accustomed to place it, he became dimly conscious of a presence or presences behind the fir wall.

He sighed deeply. No doubt the shade of his parent was restless, because—

"Fou Wang," spake a voice, low but distinct.

The young man fell upon his knees.

"Honored Mother!" he cried.

"Fou Wang," repeated the voice, "though my name is on thy lips, O'Yam's is in thy heart."

Conscience-stricken, Fou Wang yet retained spirit enough to gasp:

"Have I not been a dutiful son? Have I not sacrificed all for thee, O Mother! Why, then, dost thou reproach me?"

"I do not reproach thee," chanted three voices, and Fou Wang, lifting his head, saw three figures emerge from behind the fir wall.

"I do not reproach thee. Thou hast been a most dutiful son, and thy offerings at my grave and in the temple have been fully appreciated. Far from reproaching thee, I am here to say to thee that the dead have regard for the living who faithfully mourn and minister to them, and to bid thee sacrifice no more until thou hast satisfied thine own heart by taking to wife the daughter of Kien Lung and given to thy sister and thy sister's husband an elder brother's blessing. Thy departed mother requires not the sacrifice of a broken heart. The fallen leaf grieves not because the green leaf still clings to the bough."

Saying this, the three figures flapped the loose sleeves of the well-known garments of Ah So Nan and faded from his vision.

For a moment Fou Wang gazed after them as if spellbound. Then he arose and rushed toward the fir wall, behind which they seemed to have vanished.

"Mother, honored parent! Come back and tell me of the new birth!" he cried.

But there was no response.

Fou Wang returned to the grave and lighted the incense. But he did not wait to see its smoke ascend. Instead he hastened to the house of Kien Lung and said to the girl who met him at the door:

"No more shall my longing for thee take the fragrance from the flowers and the light from the sun and moon."

THE PRIZE CHINA BABY

The baby was the one gleam of sunshine in Fin Fan's life, and how she loved it no words can tell. When it was first born, she used to lie with her face turned to its little soft, breathing mouth and think there was nothing quite so lovely in the world as the wee pink face before her, while the touch of its tiny toes and fingers would send wonderful thrills through her whole body. Those were delightful days, but, oh, how quickly they sped. A week after the birth of the little Jessamine Flower, Fin Fan was busy winding tobacco leaves in the dark room behind her husband's factory. Winding tobacco leaves had been Fin Fan's occupation ever since she had become Chung Kee's wife, and hard and dreary work it was. Now, however, she did not mind it quite so much, for in a bunk which was built on one side of the room was a most precious bundle, and every now and then she would go over to that bunk and crow and coo to the baby therein.

But though Fin Fan prized her child so highly, Jessamine Flower's father would rather she had not been born, and considered the babe a nuisance because she took up so much of her mother's time. He would rather that Fin Fan spent the hours in winding tobacco leaves than in nursing the baby. However, Fin Fan managed to do both, and by dint of getting up very early in the morning and retiring very late at night, made as much money for her husband after the baby was born as she ever did before. And it was well for her that that was so, as the baby would otherwise have been taken from her and given to some other more fortunate woman. Not that Fin Fan considered herself unfortunate. Oh, no! She had been a hard-working little slave all her life, and after her mistress sold her to be wife to Chung Kee, she never dreamt of complaining, because, though a wife, she was still a slave.

When Jessamine Flower was about six months old one of the ladies of the Mission, in making her round of Chinatown, ran in to see Fin Fan and her baby.

"What a beautiful child!" exclaimed the lady. "And, oh, how cunning," she continued, noting the amulets on the little ankles and wrists, the tiny, quilted vest and gay little trousers in which Fin Fan had arrayed her treasure.

Fin Fan sat still and shyly smiled, rubbing her chin slowly against the baby's round cheek. Fin Fan was scarcely more than a child herself in years.

"Oh, I want to ask you, dear little mother," said the lady, "if you will not send your little one to the Chinese baby show which we are going to have on Christmas Eve in the Presbyterian Mission schoolroom."

Fin Fan's eyes brightened.

"What you think? That my baby get a prize?" she asked hesitatingly.

"I think so, indeed," answered the lady, feeling the tiny, perfectly shaped limbs and peeping into the brightest of black eyes.

From that day until Christmas Eve, Fin Fan thought of nothing but the baby show. She would be there with her baby, and if it won a prize, why, perhaps its father might be got to regard it with more favor, so that he would not frown so blackly and mutter under his breath at the slightest cry or coo.

On the morning of Christmas Eve, Chung Kee brought into Fin Fan's room a great bundle of tobacco which he declared had to be rolled by the evening, and when it was time to start for the show, the work was not nearly finished. However, Fin Fan dressed her baby, rolled it in a shawl, and with it in her arms, stealthily left the place.

It was a bright scene that greeted her upon arrival at the Mission house. The little competitors, in the enclosure that had been arranged for them, presented a peculiarly gorgeous appearance. All had been carefully prepared for the beauty test and looked as pretty

as possible, though in some cases bejeweled head dresses and volu-
minous silken garments almost hid the competitors. Some small
figures quite blazed in gold and tinsel, and then there were solemn
cherubs almost free from clothing. The majority were plump and
well-formed children, and there wasn't a cross or crying baby in the
forty-five. Fin Fan's baby made the forty-sixth, and it was immediately surrounded by a group of admiring ladies.

How Fin Fan's eyes danced. Her baby would get a prize, and she
would never more need to fear that her husband would give it away.
That terrible dread had haunted her ever since its birth. "But
surely," thought the little mother, "if it gets a prize he will be so
proud that he will let me keep it forever."

And Fin Fan's baby did get a prize—a shining gold bit—and Fin
Fan, delighted and excited, started for home. She was so happy and
proud.

—

Chung Kee was very angry. Fin Fan was not in her room, and the
work he had given her to do that morning was lying on the table
undone. He said some hard words in a soft voice, which was his way
sometimes, and then told the old woman who helped the men in the
factory to be ready to carry a baby to the herb doctor's wife that
night. "Tell her," said he, "that my cousin, the doctor, says that she
long has desired a child, and so I send her one as a Christmas present, according to American custom."

Just then came a loud knocking at the door. Chung Kee slowly
unbarred it, and two men entered, bearing a stretcher upon which a
covered form lay.

"Why be you come to my store?" asked Chung Kee in broken
English.

The men put down their burden, and one pulled down the covering from that which lay on the stretcher and revealed an unconscious woman and a dead baby.

"It was on Jackson Street. The woman was trying to run with the
baby in her arms, and just as she reached the crossing a butcher's
cart came around the corner. Some Chinese who knows you advised me to bring them here. Your wife and child, eh?"

Chung Kee stared speechlessly at the still faces—an awful horror in his eyes.

A curious crowd began to fill the place. A doctor was in the midst of it and elbowed his way to where Fin Fan was beginning to regain consciousness.

"Move back, all of you; we want some air here!" he shouted authoritatively, and Fin Fan, roused by the loud voice, feebly raised her head, and looking straight into her husband's eyes, said:

"Chung Kee's baby got first prize. Chung Kee let Fin Fan keep baby always."

That was all. Fin Fan's eyes closed. Her head fell back beside the prize baby's—hers forever.

LIN JOHN

It was New Year's Eve. Lin John mused over the brightly burning fire. Through the beams of the roof the stars shone, far away in the deep night sky they shone down upon him, and he felt their beauty, though he had no words for it. The long braid which was wound around his head lazily uncoiled and fell down his back; his smooth young face was placid and content. Lin John was at peace with the world. Within one of his blouse sleeves lay a small bag of gold, the accumulated earnings of three years, and that gold was to release his only sister from a humiliating and secret bondage. A sense of duty done led him to dream of the To-Come. What a fortunate fellow he was to have been able to obtain profitable work, and within three years to have saved four hundred dollars! In the next three years, he might be able to establish a little business and send his sister to their parents in China to live like an honest woman. The sharp edges of his life were forgotten in the drowsy warmth and the world faded into dreamland.

The latch was softly lifted; with stealthy step a woman approached the boy and knelt beside him. By the flickering gleam of the dying fire she found that for which she searched, and hiding it in her breast swiftly and noiselessly withdrew.

Lin John arose. His spirits were light—and so were his sleeves. He reached for his bowl of rice, then set it down, and suddenly his chopsticks clattered on the floor. With hands thrust into his blouse he felt for what was not there. Thus, with bewildered eyes for a few moments. Then he uttered a low cry and his face became old and gray.

———

A large apartment, richly carpeted; furniture of dark and valuable wood artistically carved; ceiling decorated with beautiful Chinese ornaments and gold incense burners; walls hung from top to bottom with long bamboo panels covered with silk, on which were printed Chinese characters; tropical plants, on stands; heavy curtains draped over windows. This, in the heart of Chinatown. And in the midst of these surroundings a girl dressed in a robe of dark blue silk worn over a full skirt richly embroidered. The sleeves fell over hands glittering with rings, and shoes of light silk were on her feet. Her hair was ornamented with flowers made of jewels; she wore three or four pairs of bracelets; her jewel earrings were over an inch long.

The girl was fair to see in that her face was smooth and oval, eyes long and dark, mouth small and round, hair of jetty hue, and figure petite and graceful.

Hanging over a chair by her side was a sealskin sacque, such as is worn by fashionable American women. The girl eyed it admiringly and every few moments stroked the soft fur with caressing fingers.

"Pau Sang," she called.

A curtain was pushed aside and a heavy, broad-faced Chinese woman in blouse and trousers of black sateen stood revealed.

"Look," said the beauty. "I have a cloak like the American ladies. Is it not fine?"

Pau Sang nodded. "I wonder at Moy Loy," said she. "He is not in favor with the Gambling Cash Tiger and is losing money."

"Moy Loy gave it not to me. I bought it myself."

"But from whom did you obtain the money?"

"If I let out a secret, will you lock it up?"

Pau Sang smiled grimly, and her companion, sidling closer to her, said: "I took the money from my brother—it was my money; for years he had been working to make it for me, and last week he told me that he had saved four hundred dollars to pay to Moy Loy, so that I might be free. Now, what do I want to be free for? To be poor? To have no one to buy me good dinners and pretty things—to be gay no more? Lin John meant well, but he knows little. As to me, I wanted a sealskin sacque like the fine American ladies. So two moons gone by I stole away to the country and found him asleep. I did not awaken him—and for the first day of the New Year I had this cloak. See?"

———

"Heaven frowns on me," said Lin John sadly, speaking to Moy Loy. "I made the money with which to redeem my sister and I have lost it. I grieve, and I would have you say to her that for her sake, I will engage myself laboriously and conform to virtue till three more New Years have grown old, and that though I merit blame for my carelessness, yet I am faithful unto her."

And with his spade over his shoulder he shuffled away from a house, from an upper window of which a woman looked down and under her breath called "Fool!"

TIAN SHAN'S KINDRED SPIRIT

Had Tian Shan been an American and China to him a forbidden country, his daring exploits and thrilling adventures would have furnished inspiration for many a newspaper and magazine article, novel, and short story. As a hero, he would certainly have far outshone Dewey, Peary, or Cook. Being, however, a Chinese, and the forbidden country America, he was simply recorded by the American press as "a wily Oriental, who, 'by ways that are dark and tricks that are vain,' is eluding the vigilance of our brave customs officers." As to his experiences, the only one who took any particular interest in them was Fin Fan.

Fin Fan was Tian Shan's kindred spirit. She was the daughter of a Canadian Chinese storekeeper and the object of much concern to both Protestant Mission ladies and good Catholic sisters.

"I like learn talk and dress like you," she would respond to attempts to bring her into the folds, "but I not want think like you. Too much discuss." And when it was urged upon her that her father was a convert—the Mission ladies declaring, to the Protestant faith, and the nuns, to the Catholic—she would calmly answer: "That so? Well, I not my father. Beside I think my father just say he Catholic (or Protestant) for sake of be amiable to you. He good-natured man and want to please you."

This independent and original stand led Fin Fan to live, as it were, in an atmosphere of outlawry even amongst her own country-women, for all proper Chinese females in Canada and America, unless their husbands are men of influence in their own country, conform upon request to the religion of the women of the white race.

———

Fin Fan sat on her father's doorstep amusing herself with a ball of yarn and a kitten. She was a pretty girl, with the delicate features, long slanting eyes, and pouting mouth of the women of Soo Chow, to which province her dead mother had belonged.

Tian Shan came along.

"Will you come for a walk around the mountain?" asked he.

"I don't know," answered Fin Fan.

"Do!" he urged.

The walk around the mountain is enjoyable at all seasons, but particularly so in the fall of the year when the leaves on the trees are turning all colors, making the mount itself look like one big posy.

The air was fresh, sweet, and piny. As Tian Shan and Fin Fan walked, they chatted gaily—not so much of Tian Shan or Fin Fan as of the brilliant landscape, the sun shining through a grove of black-trunked trees with golden leaves, the squirrels that whisked past them, the birds twittering and soliloquizing over their vanishing homes, and many other objects of nature. Tian Shan's roving life had made him quite a woodsman, and Fin Fan—well, Fin Fan was his kindred spirit.

A large oak, looking like a smoldering pyre, invited them to a seat under its boughs.

After happily munching half a dozen acorns, Fin Fan requested to be told all about Tian Shan's last adventure. Every time he crossed the border, he was obliged to devise some new scheme by which to accomplish his object, and as he usually succeeded, there was always a new story to tell whenever he returned to Canada.

This time he had run across the river a mile above the Lachine Rapids in an Indian war canoe, and landed in a cove surrounded by reefs, where pursuit was impossible. It had been a perilous undertaking, for he had had to make his way right through the swift current of the St. Lawrence, the turbulent rapids so near that it seemed as if indeed he must yield life to the raging cataract. But with in-domitable courage he had forged ahead, the canoe, with every plunge of his paddles, rising on the swells and cutting through the whitecaps, until at last he reached the shore for which he had risked so much.

Fin Fan was thoughtful for a few moments after listening to his narration.

"Why," she queried at last, "when you can make so much more money in the States than in Canada, do you come so often to this side and endanger your life as you do when returning?"

Tian Shan was puzzled himself. He was not accustomed to ana-lyzing the motives for his actions.

Seeing that he remained silent, Fin Fan went on:

"I think," said she, "that it is very foolish of you to keep running backward and forward from one country to another, wasting your time and accomplishing nothing."

Tian Shan dug up some soft, black earth with the heels of his boots.

"Perhaps it is," he observed.

That night Tian Shan's relish for his supper was less keen than usual, and when he laid his head upon his pillow, instead of sleep-ing, he could only think of Fin Fan. Fin Fan! Fin Fan! Her face was before him, her voice in his ears. The clock ticked Fin Fan; the cat purred it; a little mouse squeaked it; a night-bird sang it. He tossed about, striving to think what ailed him. With the first glimmer of morning came knowledge of his condition. He loved Fin Fan, even as the American man loves the girl he would make his wife.

Now Tian Shan, unlike most Chinese, had never saved money and, therefore, had no home to offer Fin Fan. He knew, also, that her father had his eye upon a young merchant in Montreal, who would make a very desirable son-in-law.

In the early light of the morning Tian Shan arose and wrote a letter. In this letter, which was written with a pointed brush on long yellow sheets of paper, he told Fin Fan that, as she thought it was foolish, he was going to relinquish the pleasure of running backward and forward across the border, for some time at least. He was possessed of a desire to save money so that he could have a wife and a home. In a year, perhaps, he would see her again.

———

Lee Ping could hardly believe that his daughter was seriously opposed to becoming the wife of such a good-looking, prosperous young merchant as Wong Ling. He tried to bring her to reason, but instead of yielding her will to the parental, she declared that she would take a place as a domestic to some Canadian lady with whom she had become acquainted at the Mission sooner than wed the man her father had chosen.

"Is not Wong Ling a proper man?" inquired the amazed parent.

"Whether he is proper or improper makes no difference to me," returned Fin Fan. "I will not marry him, and the law in this country is so that you cannot compel me to wed against my will."

Lee Ping's good-natured face became almost pitiful as he regarded his daughter. Only a hen who has hatched a duckling and sees it take to the water for the first time could have worn such an expression.

Fin Fan's heart softened. She was as fond of her father as he of her. Sidling up to him, she began stroking his sleeve in a coaxing fashion.

"For a little while longer I wish only to stay with you," said she.

Lee Ping shook his head, but gave in.

"You must persuade her yourself," said he to Wong Ling that evening. "We are in a country where the sacred laws and customs of China are as naught."

So Wong Ling pressed his own suit. He was not a bad-looking fellow, and knew well also how to honey his speech. Moreover, he believed in paving his way with offerings of flowers, trinkets, sweetmeats.

Fin Fan looked, listened, and accepted. Every gift that could be kept was carefully put by in a trunk which she hoped someday to take to New York. "They will help to furnish Tian Shan's home," said she.

———

Twelve moons had gone by since Tian Shan had begun to think of saving and once again he was writing to Fin Fan.

"I have made and I have saved," wrote he. "Shall I come for you?"

And by return mail came an answer which was not "No."

Of course, Fin Fan's heart beat high with happiness when Tian Shan walked into her father's store; but to gratify some indescribable feminine instinct she simply nodded coolly in his direction, and continued what might be called a flirtation with Wong Ling, who had that morning presented her with the first Chinese lily of the season and a box of the best preserved ginger.

Tian Shan sat himself down on a box of dried mushrooms and glowered at his would-be rival, who, unconscious of the fact that he was making a third when there was needed but a two, chattered on like a running stream. Thoughtlessly and kittenishly Fin Fan tossed a word, first to this one, and next to that; and whilst loving with all her heart one man, showed much more favor to the other.

Finally Tian Shan arose from the mushrooms and marched over to the counter.

"These yours?" he inquired of Wong Ling, indicating the lily and the box of ginger.

"Miss Fin Fan has done me the honor of accepting them," blandly replied Wong Ling.

"Very good," commented Tian Shan. He picked up the gifts and hurled them into the street.

A scene of wild disorder followed. In the midst of it the father of Fin Fan, who had been downtown, appeared at the door.

"What is the meaning of this?" he demanded.

"Oh, Father, Father, they are killing one another! Separate them, oh, separate them!" pleaded Fin Fan.

But her father's interference was not needed. Wong Ling swerved to one side, and falling, struck the iron foot of the stove. Tian Shan, seeing his rival unconscious, rushed out of the store.

———

The moon hung in the sky like a great yellow pearl and the night was beautiful and serene. But Fin Fan, miserable and unhappy, could not rest.

"All your fault! All your fault!" declared the voice of conscience.

"Fin Fan," spoke a voice near to her.

Could it be? Yes, it surely was Tian Shan.

She could not refrain from a little scream.

"Sh! Sh!" bade Tian Shan. "Is he dead?"

"No," replied Fin Fan, "he is very sick, but he will recover."

"I might have been a murderer," mused Tian Shan. "As it is I am liable to arrest and imprisonment for years."

"I am the cause of all the trouble," wept Fin Fan.

Tian Shan patted her shoulder in an attempt at consolation, but a sudden footfall caused her to start away from him.

"They are hunting you!" she cried. "Go! Go!"

And Tian Shan, casting upon her one long farewell look, strode with rapid steps away.

—

Poor Fin Fan! She had indeed lost everyone, and added to that shame was the secret sorrow and remorse of her own heart. All the hopes and the dreams which had filled the year that was gone were now as naught, and he, around whom they had been woven, was, because of her, a fugitive from justice, even in Canada.

One day she picked up an American newspaper which a customer had left on the counter, and, more as a habit than for any other reason, began spelling out the paragraphs.

A Chinese, who has been unlawfully breathing United States air for several years, was captured last night crossing the border, a feat which he is said to have successfully accomplished more than a dozen times during the last few years. His name is Tian Shan, and there is no doubt whatever that he will be deported to China as soon as the necessary papers can be made out.

Fin Fan lifted her head. Fresh air and light had come into her soul. Her eyes sparkled. In the closet behind her hung a suit of her father's clothes. Fin Fan was a tall and well-developed young woman.

—

"You are to have company," said the guard, pausing in front of Tian Shan's cage. "A boy without certificate was caught this morning by two of our men this side of Rouse's Point. He has been unable to give an account of himself, so we are putting him in here with you. You will probably take the trip to China together."

Tian Shan continued reading a Chinese paper which he had been allowed to retain. He was not at all interested in the companion thrust upon him. He would have preferred to be left alone. The face of the absent one is so much easier conjured in silence and solitude. It was a foregone conclusion with Tian Shan that he would never again behold Fin Fan, and with true Chinese philosophy he had begun to reject realities and accept dreams as the stuff upon which to live. Life itself was hard, bitter, and disappointing. Only dreams are joyous and smiling.

One star after another had appeared until the heavens were patterned with twinkling lights. Through his prison bars Tian Shan gazed solemnly upon the firmament.

Someone touched his elbow. It was his fellow prisoner.

So far the boy had not intruded himself, having curled himself up in a corner of the cell and slept soundly apparently, ever since his advent.

"What do you want?" asked Tian Shan not unkindly.

"To go to China with you and to be your wife," was the softly surprising reply.

"Fin Fan!" exclaimed Tian Shan. "Fin Fan!"

The boy pulled off his cap.

"Aye," said he. "'Tis Fin Fan!"

THE SING SONG WOMAN

I

Ah Oi, the Chinese actress, threw herself down on the floor of her room and, propping her chin on her hands, gazed up at the narrow strip of blue sky which could be seen through her window. She seemed to have lost her usually merry spirits. For the first time since she had left her home her thoughts were seriously with the past, and she longed with a great longing for the Chinese Sea, the boats, and the wet, blowing sands. She had been a fisherman's daughter, and many a spring had she watched the gathering of the fishing fleet to which her father's boat belonged. Well could she remember clapping her hands as the vessels steered out to sea for the season's work, her father's amongst them, looking as bright as paint could make it, and flying a neat little flag at its stern; and well could she also remember how her mother had taught her to pray to "Our Lady of Pootoo," the goddess of sailors. One does not need to be a Christian to be religious, and Ah Oi's parents had carefully instructed their daughter according to their light, and it was not their fault if their daughter was a despised actress in an American Chinatown.

The sound of footsteps outside her door seemed to chase away Ah Oi's melancholy mood, and when a girl crossed her threshold, she was gazing amusedly into the street below—a populous thoroughfare of Chinatown.

The newcomer presented a strange appearance. She was crying so hard that red paint, white powder, and carmine lip salve were all besmeared over a naturally pretty face.

Ah Oi began to laugh.

"Why, Mag-gee," said she, "how odd you look with little red rivers running over your face! What is the matter?"

"What is the matter?" echoed Mag-gee, who was a half-white girl. "The matter is that I wish that I were dead! I am to be married tonight to a Chinaman whom I have never seen, and whom I can't bear. It isn't natural that I should. I always took to other men, and never could put up with a Chinaman. I was born in America, and I'm not Chinese in looks nor in any other way. See! My eyes are blue, and there is gold in my hair; and I love potatoes and beef, and every time I eat rice it makes me sick, and so does chopped up food. He came down about a week ago and made arrangements with father, and now everything is fixed and I'm going away forever to live in China. I shall be a Chinese woman next year—I commenced to be one today, when father made me put the paint and powder on my face, and dress in Chinese clothes. Oh! I never want anyone to feel as I do. To think of having to marry a Chinaman! How I hate the Chinese! And the worst of it is, loving somebody else all the while."

The girl burst into passionate sobs. The actress, who was evidently accustomed to hearing her compatriots reviled by the white and half-white denizens of Chinatown, laughed—a light, rippling laugh. Her eyes glinted mischievously.

"Since you do not like the Chinese men," said she, "why do you give yourself to one? And if you care so much for somebody else, why do you not fly to that somebody?"

Bold words for a Chinese woman to utter! But Ah Oi was not as other Chinese women, who all their lives have been sheltered by a husband's or father's care.

The half-white girl stared at her companion.

"What do you mean?" she asked.

"This," said Ah Oi. The fair head and dark head drew near together; and two women passing the door heard whispers and suppressed laughter.

"Ah Oi is up to some trick," said one.

II

"The Sing Song Woman! The Sing Song Woman!" It was a wild cry of anger and surprise.

The ceremony of unveiling the bride had just been performed, and Hwuy Yen, the father of Mag-gee, and his friends, were in a state of great excitement, for the unveiled, brilliantly clothed little figure standing in the middle of the room was not the bride who was to have been; but Ah Oi, the actress, the Sing Song Woman.

Every voice but one was raised. The bridegroom, a tall, handsome man, did not understand what had happened, and could find no words to express his surprise at the uproar. But he was so newly wedded that it was not until Hwuy Yen advanced to the bride and shook his hand threateningly in her face, that he felt himself a husband, and interfered by placing himself before the girl.

"What is all this?" he inquired. "What has my wife done to merit such abuse?"

"Your wife!" scornfully ejaculated Hwuy Yen. "She is no wife of yours. You were to have married my daughter, Mag-gee. This is not my daughter; this is an impostor, an actress, a Sing Song Woman. Where is my daughter?"

Ah Oi laughed her peculiar, rippling, amused laugh. She was in no wise abashed, and, indeed, appeared to be enjoying the situation. Her bright, defiant eyes met her questioner's boldly as she answered:

"Mag-gee has gone to eat beef and potatoes with a white man. Oh, we had such a merry time making this play!"

"See how worthless a thing she is," said Hwuy Yen to the young bridegroom.

The latter regarded Ah Oi compassionately. He was a man, and perhaps a little tenderness crept into his heart for the girl toward whom so much bitterness was evinced. She was beautiful. He drew near to her.

"Can you not justify yourself?" he asked sadly.

For a moment Ah Oi gazed into his eyes—the only eyes that had looked with true kindness into hers for many a moon.

"You justify me," she replied with an upward, pleading glance.

Then Ke Leang, the bridegroom, spoke. He said: "The daughter of Hwuy Yen cared not to become my bride and has sought her happiness with another. Ah Oi, having a kind heart, helped her to that happiness, and tried to recompense me my loss by giving me herself. She has been unwise and indiscreet; but the good that is in her is more than the evil, and now that she is my wife, none shall say a word against her."

Ah Oi pulled at his sleeve.

"You give me credit for what I do not deserve," said she. "I had no kind feelings. I thought only of mischief, and I am not your wife. It is but a play like the play I shall act tomorrow."

"Hush!" bade Ke Leang. "You shall act no more. I will marry you again and take you to China."

Then something in Ah Oi's breast, which for a long time had been hard as stone, became soft and tender, and her eyes ran over with tears.

"Oh, sir," said she, "it takes a heart to make a heart, and you have put one today in the bosom of a Sing Song Woman."

LEAVES FROM THE MENTAL PORTFOLIO OF AN EURASIAN

When I look back over the years I see myself, a little child of scarcely four years of age, walking in front of my nurse, in a green English lane, and listening to her tell another of her kind that my mother is Chinese. "Oh, Lord!" exclaims the informed. She turns me around and scans me curiously from head to foot. Then the two women whisper together. Tho the word "Chinese" conveys very little meaning to my mind, I feel that they are talking about my father and mother and my heart swells with indignation. When we reach home I rush to my mother and try to tell her what I have heard. I am a young child. I fail to make myself intelligible. My mother does not understand, and when the nurse declares to her, "Little Miss Sui is a story-teller," my mother slaps me.

Many a long year has passed over my head since that day—the day on which I first learned that I was something different and apart from other children, but tho my mother has forgotten it, I have not.

I see myself again, a few years older. I am playing with another child in a garden. A girl passes by outside the gate. "Mamie," she cries to my companion. "I wouldn't speak to Sui if I were you. Her mamma is Chinese."

"I don't care," answers the little one beside me. And then to me, "Even if your mamma is Chinese, I like you better than I like Annie."

"But I don't like you," I answer, turning my back on her. It is my first conscious lie.

I am at a children's party, given by the wife of an Indian officer whose children were schoolfellows of mine. I am only six years of age, but have attended a private school for over a year, and have already learned that China is a heathen country, being civilized by England. However, for the time being, I am a merry romping child. There are quite a number of grown people present. One, a white-haired old man, has his attention called to me by the hostess. He adjusts his eyeglasses and surveys me critically. "Ah, indeed!" he exclaims. "Who would have thought it at first glance. Yet now I see the difference between her and other children. What a peculiar coloring! Her mother's eyes and hair and her father's features, I presume. Very interesting little creature!"

I had been called from my play for the purpose of inspection. I do not return to it. For the rest of the evening I hide myself behind a hall door and refuse to show myself until it is time to go home.

My parents have come to America. We are in Hudson City, N.Y., and we are very poor. I am out with my brother, who is ten months older than myself. We pass a Chinese store, the door of which is open. "Look!" says Charlie. "Those men in there are Chinese!" Eagerly I gaze into the long low room. With the exception of my mother, who is English bred with English ways and manner of dress, I have never seen a Chinese person. The two men within the store are uncouth specimens of their race, drest in working blouses and pantaloons with queues hanging down their backs. I recoil with a sense of shock.

"Oh, Charlie," I cry. "Are we like that?"

"Well, we're Chinese, and they're Chinese, too, so we must be!" returns my seven-year-old brother.

"Of course you are," puts in a boy who has followed us down the street, and who lives near us and has seen my mother: "Chinky, Chinky, Chinaman, yellow-face, pig-tail, rat-eater." A number of other boys and several little girls join in with him.

"Better than you," shouts my brother, facing the crowd. He is younger and smaller than any there, and I am even more insignificant than he; but my spirit revives.

"I'd rather be Chinese than anything else in the world," I scream.

They pull my hair, they tear my clothes, they scratch my face, and all but lame my brother; but the white blood in our veins fights valiantly for the Chinese half of us. When it is all over, exhausted and bedraggled, we crawl home, and report to our mother that we have "won the battle."

"Are you sure?" asks my mother doubtfully.

"Of course. They ran from us. They were frightened," returns my brother.

My mother smiles with satisfaction.

"Do you hear?" she asks my father.

"Umm," he observes, raising his eyes from his paper for an instant. My childish instinct, however, tells me that he is more interested than he appears to be.

It is tea time, but I cannot eat. Unobserved I crawl away. I do not sleep that night. I am too excited and I ache all over. Our opponents had been so very much stronger and bigger than we. Toward morning, however, I fall into a doze from which I awake myself, shouting:

"Sound the battle cry;
See the foe is nigh."

My mother believes in sending us to Sunday school. She has been brought up in a Presbyterian college.

The scene of my life shifts to eastern Canada. The sleigh which has carried us from the station stops in front of a little French Canadian hotel. Immediately we are surrounded by a number of villagers, who stare curiously at my mother as my father assists her to alight from the sleigh. Their curiosity, however, is tempered with kindness, as they watch, one after another, the little black heads of my brothers and sisters and myself emerge out of the buffalo robe, which is part of the sleigh's outfit. There are six of us, four girls and two boys; the eldest, my brother, being only seven years of age. My father and mother are still in their twenties. "Les pauvres enfants," the inhabitants murmur, as they help to carry us into the hotel. Then in lower tones: "Chinoise, Chinoise."

For some time after our arrival, whenever we children are sent for a walk, our footsteps are dogged by a number of young French and English Canadians, who amuse themselves with speculations as to whether we, being Chinese, are susceptible to pinches and hair pulling, while older persons pause and gaze upon us, very much in the same way that I have seen people gaze upon strange animals in a menagerie. Now and then we are stopped and plied with questions as to what we eat and drink, how we go to sleep, if my mother understands what my father says to her, if we sit on chairs or squat on floors, etc., etc., etc.

There are many pitched battles, of course, and we seldom leave the house without being armed for conflict. My mother takes a great interest in our battles, and usually cheers us on, tho I doubt whether she understands the depth of the troubled waters thru which her little children wade. As to my father, peace is his motto, and he deems it wisest to be blind and deaf to many things.

School days are short, but memorable. I am in the same class with my brother, my sister next to me in the class below. The little girl whose desk my sister shares shrinks close against the wall as my sister takes her place. In a little while she raises her hand.

"Please, teacher!"

"Yes, Annie."

"May I change my seat?"

"No, you may not!"

The little girl sobs. "Why should I have to sit beside a——"

Happily my sister does not seem to hear, and before long the two little girls become great friends. I have many such experiences.

My brother is remarkably bright; my sister next to me has a wonderful head for figures, and when only eight years of age helps my father with his night work accounts. My parents compare her with me. She is of sturdier build than I, and, as my father says, "Always has her wits about her." He thinks her more like my mother, who is very bright and interested in every little detail of practical life. My father tells me that I will never make half the woman that my mother is or that my sister will be. I am not as strong as my sisters, which makes me feel somewhat ashamed, for I am the eldest little girl, and more is expected of me. I have no organic disease, but the strength of my feelings seems to take from me the strength of my body. I am prostrated at times with attacks of nervous sickness. The doctor says that my heart is unusually large; but in the light of the present I know that the cross of the Eurasian bore too heavily upon my childish shoulders. I usually hide my weakness from the family until I cannot stand. I do not understand myself, and I have an idea that the others will despise me for not being as strong as they. Therefore, I like to wander away alone, either by the river or in the bush. The green fields and flowing water have a charm for me. At the age of seven, as it is today, a bird on the wing is my emblem of happiness.

I have come from a race on my mother's side which is said to be the most stolid and insensible to feeling of all races, yet I look back over the years and see myself so keenly alive to every shade of sorrow and suffering that it is almost a pain to live.

If there is any trouble in the house in the way of a difference between my father and mother, or if any child is punished, how I suffer! And when harmony is restored, heaven seems to be around me. I can be sad, but I can also be glad. My mother's screams of agony when a baby is born almost drive me wild, and long after her pangs have subsided I feel them in my own body. Sometimes it is a week before I can get to sleep after such an experience.

A debt owing by my father fills me with shame. I feel like a criminal when I pass the creditor's door. I am only ten years old. And all the while the question of nationality perplexes my little brain. Why are we what we are? I and my brothers and sisters. Why did God make us to be hooted and stared at? Papa is English, mamma is Chinese. Why couldn't we have been either one thing or the other? Why is my mother's race despised? I look into the faces of my father and mother. Is she not every bit as dear and good as he? Why? Why? She sings us the songs she learned at her English school. She tells us tales of China. Tho a child when she left her native land she remembers it well, and I am never tired of listening to the story of how she was stolen from her home. She tells us over and over again of her meeting with my father in Shanghai and the romance of their marriage. Why? Why?

I do not confide in my father and mother. They would not understand. How could they? He is English, she is Chinese. I am different to both of them—a stranger, tho their own child. "What are we?" I ask my brother. "It doesn't matter, sissy," he responds. But it does. I love poetry, particularly heroic pieces. I also love fairy tales. Stories of everyday life do not appeal to me. I dream dreams of being great and noble; my sisters and brothers also. I glory in the idea of dying at the stake and a great genie arising from the flames and declaring to those who have scorned us: "Behold, how great and glorious and noble are the Chinese people!"

My sisters are apprenticed to a dressmaker; my brother is entered in an office. I tramp around and sell my father's pictures, also some lace which I make myself. My nationality, if I had only known it at that time, helps to make sales. The ladies who are my customers call me "The Little Chinese Lace Girl." But it is a dangerous life for a very young girl. I come near to "mysteriously disappearing" many a time. The greatest temptation was in the thought of getting far away from where I was known, to where no mocking cries of "Chinese!" "Chinese!" could reach.

Whenever I have the opportunity I steal away to the library and read every book I can find on China and the Chinese. I learn that China is the oldest civilized nation on the face of the earth and a few other things. At eighteen years of age what troubles me is not that I am what I am, but that others are ignorant of my superiority. I am small, but my feelings are big—and great is my vanity.

My sisters attend dancing classes, for which they pay their own fees. In spite of covert smiles and sneers, they are glad to meet and mingle with other young folk. They are not sensitive in the sense that I am. And yet they understand. One of them tells me that she overheard a young man say to another that he would rather marry a pig than a girl with Chinese blood in her veins.

In course of time I too learn shorthand and take a position in an office. Like my sister, I teach myself, but, unlike my sister, I have neither the perseverance nor the ability to perfect myself. Besides, to a temperament like mine, it is torture to spend the hours in transcribing other people's thoughts. Therefore, altho I can always earn a moderately good salary, I do not distinguish myself in the business world as does she.

When I have been working for some years I open an office of my own. The local papers patronize me and give me a number of assignments, including most of the local Chinese reporting. I meet many Chinese persons, and when they get into trouble am often called upon to fight their battles in the papers. This I enjoy. My heart leaps for joy when I read one day an article signed by a New York Chinese in which he declares "The Chinese in America owe an everlasting debt of gratitude to Sui Sin Far for the bold stand she has taken in their defense."

The Chinaman who wrote the article seeks me out and calls upon me. He is a clever and witty man, a graduate of one of the American colleges and as well a Chinese scholar. I learn that he has an American wife and several children. I am very much interested in these children, and when I meet them my heart throbs in sympathetic tune with the tales they relate of their experiences as Eurasians. "Why did papa and mamma born us?" asks one. Why?

I also meet other Chinese men who compare favorably with the white men of my acquaintance in mind and heart qualities. Some of them are quite handsome. They have not as finely cut noses and as well-developed chins as the white men, but they have smoother skins and their expression is more serene; their hands are better shaped and their voices softer.

Some little Chinese women whom I interview are very anxious to know whether I would marry a Chinaman. I do not answer No. They clap their hands delightedly, and assure me that the Chinese are much the finest and best of all men. They are, however, a little doubtful as to whether one could be persuaded to care for me, full-blooded Chinese people having a prejudice against the half white.

Fundamentally, I muse, all people are the same. My mother's race is as prejudiced as my father's. Only when the whole world becomes as one family will human beings be able to see clearly and hear distinctly. I believe that someday a great part of the world will be Eurasian. I cheer myself with the thought that I am but a pioneer. A pioneer should glory in suffering.

"You were walking with a Chinaman yesterday," accuses an acquaintance.

"Yes, what of it?"

"You ought not to. It isn't right."

"Not right to walk with one of my own mother's people? Oh, indeed!"

I cannot reconcile his notion of righteousness with my own.

———

I am living in a little town away off on the north shore of a big lake. Next to me at the dinner table is the man for whom I work as a stenographer. There are also a couple of businessmen, a young girl, and her mother.

Someone makes a remark about the cars full of Chinamen that passed that morning. A transcontinental railway runs thru the town.

My employer shakes his rugged head. "Somehow or other," says he, "I cannot reconcile myself to the thought that the Chinese are humans like ourselves. They may have immortal souls, but their faces seem to be so utterly devoid of expression that I cannot help but doubt."

"Souls," echoes the town clerk. "Their bodies are enough for me. A Chinaman is, in my eyes, more repulsive than a nigger."

"They always give me such a creepy feeling," puts in the young girl with a laugh.

"I wouldn't have one in my house," declares my landlady.

"Now, the Japanese are different altogether. There is something bright and likeable about those men," continues Mr. K.

A miserable, cowardly feeling keeps me silent. I am in a Middle West town. If I declare what I am, every person in the place will hear about it the next day. The population is in the main made up of working folks with strong prejudices against my mother's countrymen. The prospect before me is not an enviable one—if I speak. I have no longer an ambition to die at the stake for the sake of demonstrating the greatness and nobleness of the Chinese people.

Mr. K. turns to me with a kindly smile.

"What makes Miss Far so quiet?" he asks.

"I don't suppose she finds the 'washee washee men' particularly interesting subjects of conversation," volunteers the young manager of the local bank.

With a great effort I raise my eyes from my plate. "Mr. K.," I say, addressing my employer, "the Chinese people may have no souls, no expression on their faces, be altogether beyond the pale of civilization, but whatever they are, I want you to understand that I am—I am a Chinese."

There is silence in the room for a few minutes. Then Mr. K. pushes back his plate and standing up beside me, says:

"I should not have spoken as I did. I know nothing whatever about the Chinese. It was pure prejudice. Forgive me!"

I admire Mr. K.'s moral courage in apologizing to me; he is a conscientious Christian man, but I do not remain much longer in the little town.

———

I am under a tropic sky, meeting frequently and conversing with persons who are almost as high up in the world as birth, education, and money can set them. The environment is peculiar, for I am also surrounded by a race of people, the reputed descendants of Ham, the son of Noah, whose offspring, it was prophesied, should be the servants of the sons of Shem and Japheth. As I am a descendant, according to the Bible, of both Shem and Japheth, I have a perfect right to set my heel upon the Ham people; but tho I see others around me following out the Bible suggestion, it is not in my nature to be arrogant to any but those who seek to impress me with their superiority, which the poor black maid who has been assigned to me by the hotel certainly does not. My employer's wife takes me to task for this. "It is unnecessary," she says, "to thank a black person for a service."

The novelty of life in the West Indian island is not without its charm. The surroundings, people, manner of living, are so entirely different from what I have been accustomed to up north that I feel as if I were "born again." Mixing with people of fashion, and yet not of them, I am not of sufficient importance to create comment or curiosity. I am busy nearly all day and often well into the night. It is not monotonous work, but it is certainly strenuous. The planters and businessmen of the island take me as a matter of course and treat me with kindly courtesy. Occasionally an Englishman will warn me against the "brown boys" of the island, little dreaming that I too am of the "brown people" of the earth.

When it begins to be whispered about the place that I am not all white, some of the "sporty" people seek my acquaintance. I am small and look much younger than my years. When, however, they discover that I am a very serious and sober-minded spinster indeed, they retire quite gracefully, leaving me a few amusing reflections.

One evening a card is brought to my room. It bears the name of some naval officer. I go down to my visitor, thinking he is probably someone who, having been told that I am a reporter for the local paper, has brought me an item of news. I find him lounging in an easy chair on the veranda of the hotel—a big, blond, handsome fellow, several years younger than I.

"You are Lieutenant———?" I inquire.

He bows and laughs a little. The laugh doesn't suit him somehow—and it doesn't suit me, either.

"If you have anything to tell me, please tell it quickly, because I'm very busy."

"Oh, you don't really mean that," he answers, with another silly and offensive laugh. "There's always plenty of time for good times. That's what I am here for. I saw you at the races the other day and twice at King's House. My ship will be here for——weeks."

"Do you wish that noted?" I ask.

"Oh, no! Why—I came just because I had an idea that you might like to know me. I would like to know you. You look such a nice little body. Say, wouldn't you like to go out for a sail this lovely night? I will tell you all about the sweet little Chinese girls I met when we were at Hong Kong. They're not so shy!"

———

I leave eastern Canada for the Far West, so reduced by another attack of rheumatic fever that I only weigh eighty-four pounds. I travel on an advertising contract. It is presumed by the railway company that in some way or other I will give them full value for their transportation across the continent. I have been ordered beyond the Rockies by the doctor, who declares that I will never regain my strength in the East. Nevertheless, I am but two days in San Francisco when I start out in search of work. It is the first time that I have sought work as a stranger in a strange town. Both of the other positions away from home were secured for me by home influence. I am quite surprised to find that there is no demand for my services in San Francisco and that no one is particularly interested in me. The best I can do is to accept an offer from a railway agency to typewrite their correspondence for $5 a month. I stipulate, however, that I shall have the privilege of taking in outside work and that my hours shall be light. I am hopeful that the sale of a story or newspaper article may add to my income, and I console myself with the reflection that, considering that I still limp and bear traces of sickness, I am fortunate to secure any work at all.

The proprietor of one of the San Francisco papers, to whom I have a letter of introduction, suggests that I obtain some subscriptions from the people of Chinatown, that district of the city having never been canvassed. This suggestion I carry out with enthusiasm, tho I find that the Chinese merchants and people generally are inclined to regard me with suspicion. They have been imposed upon so many times by unscrupulous white people. Another drawback— save for a few phrases, I am unacquainted with my mother tongue. How, then, can I expect these people to accept me as their own countrywoman? The Americanized Chinamen actually laugh in my face when I tell them that I am of their race. However, they are not all "doubting Thomases." Some little women discover that I have Chinese hair, color of eyes and complexion, also that I love rice and tea. This settles the matter for them—and for their husbands.

My Chinese instincts develop. I am no longer the little girl who shrunk against my brother at the first sight of a Chinaman. Many and many a time, when alone in a strange place, has the appearance of even a humble laundryman given me a sense of protection and made me feel quite at home. This fact of itself proves to me that prejudice can be eradicated by association.

I meet a half-Chinese, half-white girl. Her face is plastered with a thick white coat of paint and her eyelids and eyebrows are blackened so that the shape of her eyes and the whole expression of her face is changed. She was born in the East, and at the age of eighteen came West in answer to an advertisement. Living for many years among the working class, she had heard little but abuse of the Chinese. It is not difficult, in a land like California, for a half-Chinese, half-white girl to pass as one of Spanish or Mexican origin. This the poor child does, tho she lives in nervous dread of being "discovered." She becomes engaged to a young man, but fears to tell him what she is, and only does so when compelled by a fearless American girlfriend. This girl, who knows her origin, realizing that the truth sooner or later must be told, and better soon than late, advises the Eurasian to confide in the young man, assuring her that he loves her well enough not to allow her nationality to stand, a bar sinister, between them. But the Eurasian prefers to keep her secret, and only reveals it to the man who is to be her husband when driven to by the American girl, who declares that if the half-breed will not tell the truth she will. When the young man hears that the girl he is engaged to has Chinese blood in her veins, he exclaims: "Oh, what will my folks say?" But that is all. Love is stronger than prejudice with him, and neither he nor she deems it necessary to inform his "folks."

The Americans, having for many years manifested a much higher regard for the Japanese than for the Chinese, several half-Chinese young men and women, thinking to advance themselves, both in a social and business sense, pass as Japanese. They continue to be known as Eurasians; but a Japanese Eurasian does not appear in the same light as a Chinese Eurasian. The unfortunate Chinese Eurasians! Are not those who compel them to thus cringe more to be blamed than they?

People, however, are not all alike. I meet white men, and women, too, who are proud to mate with those who have Chinese blood in their veins, and think it a great honor to be distinguished by the friendship of such. There are also Eurasians and Eurasians. I know of one who allowed herself to become engaged to a white man after refusing him nine times. She had discouraged him in every way possible, had warned him that she was half Chinese; that her people were poor, that every week or month she sent home a certain amount of her earnings, and that the man she married would have to do as much, if not more; also, most uncompromising truth of all, that she did not love him and never would. But the resolute and undaunted lover swore that it was a matter of indifference to him whether she was a Chinese or a Hottentot, that it would be his plea-sure and privilege to allow her relations double what it was in her power to bestow, and as to not loving him—that did not matter at all. He loved her. So, because the young woman had a married mother and married sisters, who were always picking at her and gossiping over her independent manner of living, she finally con-sented to marry him, recording the agreement in her diary thus:

"I have promised to become the wife of _____ on _____, 189 , because the world is so cruel and sneering to a single woman—and for no other reason."

Everything went smoothly until one day. The young man was driving a pair of beautiful horses and she was seated by his side, try-ing very hard to imagine herself in love with him, when a Chinese vegetable gardener's cart came rumbling along. The Chinaman was a jolly-looking individual in blue cotton blouse and pantaloons, his rakish-looking hat being kept in place by a long queue which was pulled upward from his neck and wound around it. The young woman was suddenly possessed with the spirit of mischief. "Look!" she cried, indicating the Chinaman, "there's my brother. Why don't you salute him?"

The man's face fell a little. He sank into a pensive mood. The wicked one by his side read him like an open book.

"When we are married," said she, "I intend to give a Chinese party every month."

No answer.

"As there are very few aristocratic Chinese in this city, I shall fill up with the laundrymen and vegetable farmers. I don't believe in being exclusive in democratic America, do you?"

He hadn't a grain of humor in his composition, but a sickly smile contorted his features as he replied:

"You shall do just as you please, my darling. But—but—consider a moment. Wouldn't it be just a little pleasanter for us if, after we are married, we allowed it to be presumed that you were—er—Japanese? So many of my friends have inquired of me if that is not your nationality. They would be so charmed to meet a little Japanese lady."

"Hadn't you better oblige them by finding one?"

"Why—er—what do you mean?"

"Nothing much in particular. Only—I am getting a little tired of this," taking off his ring.

"You don't mean what you say! Oh, put it back, dearest! You know I would not hurt your feelings for the world!"

"You haven't. I'm more than pleased. But I do mean what I say."

That evening the "ungrateful" Chinese Eurasian diaried, among other things, the following:

"Joy, oh, joy! I'm free once more. Never again shall I be untrue to my own heart. Never again will I allow anyone to 'hound' or 'sneer' me into matrimony."

I secure transportation to many California points. I meet some literary people, chief among whom is the editor of the magazine who took my first Chinese stories. He and his wife give me a warm welcome to their ranch. They are broad-minded people, whose interest in me is sincere and intelligent, not affected and vulgar. I also meet some funny people who advise me to "trade" upon my nationality. They tell me that if I wish to succeed in literature in America I should dress in Chinese costume, carry a fan in my hand, wear a pair of scarlet beaded slippers, live in New York, and come of high birth. Instead of making myself familiar with the Chinese-Americans around me, I should discourse on my spirit acquaintance with Chinese ancestors and quote in between the "Good mornings" and "How d'ye dos" of editors,

"Confucius, Confucius, how great is Confucius, Before Confucius, there never was Confucius, After Confucius, there never came Confucius," etc., etc., etc.,"

or something like that, both illuminating and obscuring, don't you know. They forget, or perhaps they are not aware that the old Chinese sage taught "The way of sincerity is the way of heaven."

My experiences as an Eurasian never cease; but people are not now as prejudiced as they have been. In the West, too, my friends are more advanced in all lines of thought than those whom I know in eastern Canada—more genuine, more sincere, with less of the form of religion, but more of its spirit.

So I roam backward and forward across the continent. When I am East, my heart is West. When I am West, my heart is East. Before long I hope to be in China. As my life began in my father's country it may end in my mother's.

After all I have no nationality and am not anxious to claim any. Individuality is more than nationality. "You are you and I am I," says Confucius. I give my right hand to the Occidentals and my left to the Orientals, hoping that between them they will not utterly destroy the insignificant "connecting link." And that's all.

Seattle, Wash.

ABOUT THE AUTHOR

EDITH MAUDE EATON (1865–1914), who took the pen name SUI SIN FAR, was the first Asian American, man or woman, to publish fiction. The daughter of a Chinese mother and an English father, Eaton began publishing articles about Montreal's Chinese Canadian community in English-language newspapers at twenty-five. At thirty, she moved to the United States and began writing stories that countered racist portrayals of the Chinese, insisting that "only when the whole world becomes as one family will human beings be able to see clearly and hear distinctly." Eaton would devote the rest of her career to promoting the fair and equal treatment of Chinese immigrants and protesting against the United States' anti-Chinese laws and its practice of separating families. She published her collected short stories as *Mrs. Spring Fragrance and Other Writings* in 1912.

ABOUT THE TYPE

The principal text of this Modern Library edition was set in a
digitized version of Janson, a typeface that dates from about 1690
and was cut by Nicholas Kis (1650–1702), a Hungarian working in
Amsterdam. The original matrices have survived and are held by
the Stempel foundry in Germany. Hermann Zapf (1918–2015) re-
designed some of the weights and sizes for Stempel, basing his
revisions on the original design.

THE MODERN LIBRARY
TORCHBEARERS

A new series featuring women who wrote on their own terms,
with boldness, creativity, and a spirit of resistance.

The *Custom of the Country* by Edith Wharton
Lady Audley's Secret by Mary Elizabeth Braddon
Love, Anger, Madness by Marie Vieux-Chauvet
Nada by Carmen Laforet
Persuasion by Jane Austen
The Return of the Soldier by Rebecca West
The Transformation of Philip Jettan by Georgette Heyer
There Is Confusion by Jessie Redmon Fauset
Villette by Charlotte Brontë

MODERNLIBRARY.COM